HIGH PRAISE
FOR ROBERT J. RANDISI!

THREE AGAINST ONE

Lancaster had already decided that he'd have to take Quitman first, and Hennessy second. The third man was still at the horse's head, in front of the buckboard. He'd have to step clear to have a shot, but Lancaster had a split second to make his decision, and he went with it.

He lowered his pistol and fired at Quitman. The bullet struck him in the chest as he was drawing his gun. He staggered backward, his feet got tangled. And he fell onto his back, dead.

Hennessy's musculature had fooled Lancaster into thinking the man would be slow. He wasn't. He already had his gun out as Lancaster turned the shotgun on him, and Lancaster knew he was going to be too late. . . .

Robert J. Randisi

LANCASTER'S ORPHANS

LEISURE BOOKS   NEW YORK CITY

To Marthayn, who took in my orphaned heart.

LEISURE BOOKS ®

January 2004

Published by

Dorchester Publishing Co., Inc.
200 Madison Avenue
New York, NY 10016

ISBN 0-8439-5225-3

Printed in the United States of America.

Visit us on the web at www.dorchesterpub.com.

LANCASTER'S
ORPHANS

Chapter One

As soon as Lancaster rode into Council Bluffs, Iowa, he had a bad feeling. The street was filled with people, and there was a carnival atmosphere in the air. As he dismounted in front of the Black Horse Saloon the crowd kept him from seeing what was causing all the commotion, but he was more interested in getting a cold beer, anyway. The hot sun had all but baked him dry.

He entered the saloon and saw that the interior was in shambles. Chairs and tables had been overturned, there was glass everywhere, presumably from broken bottles. It was getting on toward mid-afternoon, when saloon business generally picked up, but there were only three men in this one—one

1

behind the bar, and two in front of it. Everyone else was apparently outside.

He stepped through the rubble to the bar. "Can I get a beer?"

The man behind the bar looked at the other two, one of whom nodded and shrugged.

"Why not?" the bartender asked. "Looks like we're open again."

He was a big, heavyset man in his late forties, whose face was blazing red, probably because it was almost as hot inside as it was out. The only saving grace was that they were not out in the direct sunlight.

"Open again?" Lancaster asked as the man set a frothy mug of beer in front of him.

"Yeah," the barman said, "we *were* closed for the trial."

Lancaster took two big swallows of the cold beer and shuddered. He put the mug down on the bar, determined not to make himself sick by guzzling it. He took a few seconds to get his breath back.

"What was the trial about?"

"Murder, friend," one of the other men said, "it was about murder."

Lancaster turned his attention toward the speaker. He was about the bartender's age, but smaller, thinner. Although he looked hot he did not seem to be suffering as much as the bartender. Of course, it didn't help that he was wearing a three-piece suit, which indicated to Lancaster that the man probably was high-up in the town hierarchy.

"Really? I thought by all the commotion outside that the circus might be in town."

"It is," the third man said, "in a way."

"A circus *and* a trial?" Lancaster asked.

"Well," the man said, "not so much a circus as a hanging—which sort of brings a circus atmosphere with it."

A chill went through Lancaster that had nothing to do with the beer.

"A hanging?" he asked. "So soon after the trial?"

The man in the suit looked away.

"Guilty's guilty," the third man said.

He was younger than the other two, maybe early thirties—a few years younger than Lancaster, as well. He had large circles of sweat under his arms. The gun he wore was not fancy, but it was clean and the man wore it like he knew how to use it. That was something Lancaster had trained himself to notice, and it had saved his life many times. The man had a toothpick in his mouth that he removed to speak, and then replaced.

"The town's real excited about it," the bartender said. "There hasn't been a hangin' around here in a long time."

"Then why aren't you out there?"

"I'm not interested in watching a hangin'," the bartender said.

3

"And it won't start without us," the second man said, his tone regretful.

"Why's that?" Lancaster asked.

The third man removed the toothpick from his mouth and said, "I'm the hangman." He smiled, as if the announcement pleased him, and reinserted the toothpick.

"And you?" Lancaster asked the man in the suit.

"I'm the mayor," he said, "and I presided over the trial as judge."

"And was there a jury?"

"Sure was," the third man said. "Six good and honest men." Toothpick out, toothpick in.

"And they found him guilty and sentenced him to hang . . . today?" Lancaster asked.

"That's right," the mayor said, looking away and not meeting Lancaster's eyes.

"And where's the sheriff during all this?"

The hangman took the toothpick out of his mouth, flicked it away and said, "Oh, he's the one bein' hanged."

Chapter Two

"So, in other words," Lancaster said, putting all the facts together, "it's a lynching."

"All legal and on the up-and-up," the hangman said, shaking his head.

Lancaster looked at the mayor.

"What's your name, sir?"

"Hansen," he said, "Mayor Fred Hansen."

"Mayor Hansen, are you a duly elected or appointed judge?"

"Closest thing we got to one in this town," the hangman said.

"And what's your name?"

"Quitman," the man said, "Sam Quitman."

"And what qualifies you to be a hangman, Mr. Quitman?" Lancaster asked.

5

The man took a fresh toothpick from his shirt pocket, smiled, said, "I volunteered," and stuck it in his mouth.

Lancaster wondered why anyone would volunteer for such a job, but he didn't have a chance to ask.

"Come on," Quitman said to the mayor, "we got to get it done."

Lancaster noticed that the mayor did not seem happy about it. He also noticed that, of the three men, Quitman was the only one who was armed.

" 'Scuse me," Hansen said to Lancaster, and moved past him. The angle was such that only Lancaster was able to see the pleading look in the man's eyes.

"You got somethin' else to say about all of this, Mister?" Quitman said, coming up alongside Lancaster. The other man had to look up, as he was about five inches shorter than Lancaster's six-four.

Lancaster held up his mug and said, "I just came in for a cold beer."

"Well, take my advice: Finish your beer and then move on." With that, Quitman moved past Lancaster and out of the saloon, walking in the mayor's wake.

"You got to do somethin' about this, Mister!" the bartender blurted, when they were alone.

"About what?"

"It's Quitman and his gang. They forced Mayor Hansen into this."

6

"And the townspeople? They're just going along with it?"

"They just went crazy," the bartender said. "It's hot, and Quitman incited them to have a trial and find Sheriff Lockwood guilty."

"Of what?"

The barkeep shrugged.

"Who knows?"

"They're hanging a man—a lawman—and they don't know why?"

"Quitman said he knows why, and that's enough," the bartender said. "Once the jury came back with a guilty verdict—and they didn't even leave the room—they took the sheriff down the street to get a rope. But it's Quitman who's gonna do the hangin', and once he's done that him and his men will take over the town."

"And no one will try to stop them?"

"Sheriff Lockwood was the only one with enough gumption to stand up to Quitman and his men, and look what's happening."

"He has no deputies?"

"He did, but they quit when things got rough."

"What about the jury?" Lancaster asked. "What's their part?"

"Quitman handpicked them, and they were all too scared not to find the sheriff guilty."

"How many men does Quitman have?"

"There are three of them—including him."

7

"Three men have cowed an entire town?"

"Three *killers*. I don't know why they didn't just shoot the sheriff down and be done with it, or run him out of town" the bartender said. "Why do this?"

"After it's done," Lancaster said, "they'll have a lock on this town, that's why. After it's done everyone will be too sick, and too guilty, to stand up to them."

"You got that right, Mister," the barman said, "and that's why you got to do something."

"Why me?" Lancaster asked, picking up his mug again. "I just came here for a beer. I've got no stake in this."

"You know how to use that gun," the bartender said, "I can tell by lookin' at ya."

"Is that right?"

"There ain't nobody else," the man went on. "These people have worked hard to build this town—"

"Then they should defend it," Lancaster said. "I've never known a bartender who didn't have a shotgun behind the bar. Why didn't you use it?"

"Mister," he said, "I ain't proud of it, but I'm just as scared as the rest of 'em."

"Yeah, well . . ." Lancaster said. Why should he get involved? Once he'd made his way with a gun, but accidentally shooting down a little girl—a little girl with blue eyes—had changed all that. He had only recently crawled out of the bottle, and he was trying to stay out. In fact, this beer was the first liquor he'd touched in months. "It's none of my business."

"You ever been a lawman before?" the bartender asked.

"No." The man had no idea how ironic that question was.

The bartender reached beneath the bar and came up with a dented silver star, which he set down next to Lancaster's mug.

"They tore that off the sheriff's shirt," he said. "You can be a lawman now."

"I can't just put that on and be sheriff," Lancaster contested. "That's not how it's done."

"Yes it is," the bartender said. "My name's Ted Ryan, and I'm on the town council. In the absence of any other members I form a majority, and I can appoint you temporary sheriff."

"Temporary until when?"

"Just until you save the sheriff's life."

"Or I'm shot dead trying."

Lancaster stared at the badge. All he'd wanted was a goddamned beer, first one in ages. He sure picked a hell of a time. . . .

"You know what gets me?" Ryan asked.

"What?"

"The people."

"What about them?"

"After a while they really . . . well, they really

9

wanted this lynching, you know? They got a taste for it. I don't get it, I just don't get it. I mean, they *know* Ben Lockwood, but when they dragged him out of here there was . . . a *hunger* in their eyes."

"Jesus," Lancaster said, "hand me that shotgun. . . ."

He picked up the badge, put it on, and left the saloon.

Chapter Three

As he approached the crowd he noticed that the sheriff was standing on a buckboard that was being used as a makeshift gallows, with a rope hanging from a fancy new gaslight pole. The town has gaslights, for *Chrissake*, yet they didn't have decent deputies to back up their sheriff. The lawman's hands had been tied behind his back, and the noose was already around his neck.

Lancaster was just in time.

He fired into the air one barrel of the Greener shotgun the bartender had passed him, then ejected the spent shell and inserted a fresh one as he pushed through the crowd. They moved out of his way and when he reached the buckboard he had the shotgun in one hand and his pistol in the other.

A man was holding the head of the single horse hitched to the buckboard, or else the animal would have bolted when Lancaster fired his first shot. Great, he'd almost lynched the sheriff himself, Lancaster thought.

"People, listen to me!" he shouted. "Look at what you're doing. This man is your sheriff."

"Not anymore he isn't."

Quitman stepped forward so that he was standing alongside the buckboard, facing Lancaster. The man holding the horse was apparently one of his men. He had the same look.

"Who says he isn't?" Lancaster demanded.

"The mayor."

"Mayor Hansen!" Lancaster called.

Reluctantly, the politician stepped away from the crowd.

"Mayor," Lancaster instructed, "you look up into the eyes of that man on the buckboard and tell him he's not the sheriff of your town, anymore."

Together, Lancaster and the mayor looked up at Sheriff Ben Lockwood. Lancaster saw that the man was in his thirties, tall—almost as tall as he was—and fit. His eyes were strong, boring into the mayor's until the politician was forced to look away. Lancaster instinctively knew that this man would go to his death with dignity—even at the end of a rope, perhaps the most undignified death of all.

"He's guilty!" someone shouted.

"Of what?" Lancaster called back. "Does anyone even know?" He looked into the face of a man. "You, sir, do you know?"

The man looked dumbfounded.

Lancaster picked out a respectable looking woman to attack next.

"You, ma'am, do you have any idea?"

"Why, I—I wasn't even in the saloon. I mean, the courtroom." She blushed.

"But you're here, aren't you?" he asked. "You're here to watch him dance at the end of a rope? Why?"

The woman averted her eyes.

Lancaster looked at a boy of about ten next.

"You son," he asked. "Do you know what he's guilty of?"

"No, sir."

"Then why are you here?"

The boy shrugged. "I jus' wanna see a hangin'."

"Look at all of you," Lancaster said, addressing the entire crowd now. "Look what you're teaching your children."

"Mister," Quitman said. "You're poking your nose in here where it don't belong. Pinnin' on that badge don't give you the right to do that."

"This man," Lancaster said, ignoring Quitman, "and his men want to take over your town, and this is the way they're going to do it. They incite a lynching, forcing you—no, letting you—lynch your own sheriff, your neighbor."

"We ain't doin' it!" someone shouted. "He is."

"But you're letting him," Lancaster retorted, "and you're watching. Once you let them do this, you'll be under their thumbs forever."

"This man is holdin' up a legal hangin'," Quitman shouted. "You gonna let him get away with that?"

"That's what I'm asking, too," Lancaster said, just as loudly. "Are you going to let him and his men turn you into a mindless lynch mob?"

"Mister—" Quitman started, but Lancaster cut him off.

"Let them decide for themselves, Quitman!"

"I do the decidin'," Quitman said. "Hennessy!"

Foolishly, Quitman identified his third man for Lancaster. Hennessy pushed through the crowd, a broad, well-muscled man whose face was covered with black stubble. He stepped forward until he was also alongside the buckboard. On his hip he sported a pistol in a well-worn holster. Quitman took two steps away, so he wouldn't be between Hennessy and Lancaster.

"Yeah, Sam?" Hennessy asked.

"You got another rope?"

"Sure do."

Hennessy gave Lancaster a long, appraising look.

"He's a tall one, Sam."

14

"That's okay," Quitman said. "A tall man hangs from a short rope."

"Don't move, Hennessy," Lancaster ordered.

The man froze.

"These people haven't made up their minds yet, Quitman."

"I'm makin' it up for them, friend," Quitman said. He spread his legs, adopting a belligerent stance. "You want to put your guns down and walk away now? Take off that badge and toss it into the dirt where it belongs? Or you want to hang alongside the ex-sheriff here?"

"I'm not walking away," Lancaster said, "and I don't intend to hang, so you better come up with another choice."

"You called it," Quitman said, then shouted, "Take him!"

Chapter Four

Lancaster had already decided that he'd have to take Quitman first, and Hennessy second. The third man was still at the horse's head, in front of the buckboard. He'd have to step clear to have a shot, but Lancaster had a split second to make his decision, and he went with it.

He lowered his pistol and fired at Quitman. The bullet struck him in the chest as he was drawing his gun. He staggered backward, his feet got tangled. And he fell onto his back, dead.

Hennessy's musculature had fooled Lancaster into thinking the man would be slow. He wasn't. He already had his gun out as Lancaster turned the shotgun on him, and Lancaster knew he was going to be too late. But whoever had hoisted the sheriff up onto the buckboard and tied his hands had left his feet unbound. They probably thought it would be fun to watch him kick as he died. Lockwood took one step and kicked Hennessy in the side of the head. It was an awkward move, but effective. It gave Lancaster time to level the shotgun and fire. He'd meant to fire one barrel, but in his haste fired both. Hennessy took most of the force of the buckshot in the belly. It took him off his feet and left him sprawled on the ground with most of his belly missing.

Now Lancaster swiveled to face the man who was stepping away from the horse, gun already in hand. He dropped the shotgun and both men were bringing their guns to bear at the same time. He had a fifty-fifty chance here of coming out alive, but he also knew this was bad for the sheriff, because no one was holding the horse. The animal was panicking because of all the shots and, once released, was preparing to run.

Two things happened at the same time. Lancaster fired a split second before the other man. His slug caught the man in the gut, while the other man's bullet skimmed across his left side, digging a deep bloody furrow and then continuing on. As this happened someone leaped forward from the crowd, grabbed the horse's head and fought to keep the animal from bolting.

Lancaster picked up the shotgun and stepped up

to see who had stopped the horse. He found himself looking at the ten-year-old boy he'd badgered just moments before. Apparently, it had taken all the boy's strength and weight to steady the horse.

"Good work, son," he said. "You got him?"

"I got 'im, sir."

Lancaster nodded, and climbed up onto the buckboard to stand next to the sheriff.

"Ladies and gentlemen, Sam Quitman told me he volunteered to be the hangman," he shouted out. "Well, the hangman's dead. Are there any volunteers to take his place?"

No one answered, as men and women in the crowd exchanged puzzled glances.

"Come on, come on," Lancaster said. "You all wanted to see a hanging just a few moments ago. Who's got the nerve to step up."

"You're pushing *my* luck, friend," Ben Lockwood said, out of the side of his mouth.

"They're followers," Lancaster said to the man, "not leaders." To the crowd he said, "So, no volunteers? Well then, maybe you people should go on home and think about what you almost did here today. Go on! Move!"

The crowd began to disperse as Lancaster holstered his gun, set the shotgun down, slipped the noose off the lawman's neck and untied his hands.

"Mister," Lockwood said, rubbing his wrists, "I don't know who you are, but I owe you my life."

"Here," Lancaster said, taking the badge off, "this is yours—and the only thing you owe me is a beer. It's what I came into this town to get, and I never finished it."

"Mister," the sheriff said, pinning his star back on and then putting his hand out for Lancaster to shake, "you got all the beer you want in this town."

"One," Lancaster said, "one is all I want."

Chapter Five

Lancaster walked over to the young boy who had grabbed the horse and asked, "What's your name, son?"

"Aaron."

"You did a brave thing, Aaron," Lancaster said. "You saved the sheriff's life."

"Well, you were all alone, sir," Aaron said, "and you both needed help."

Lancaster turned as the sheriff joined them.

"Sheriff, do you know Aaron?"

"No, I don't," Sheriff Lockwood said. "You must be new in town, son."

"Yes sir," Aaron said. "Just rode in today."

"Well, I owe you my life," Lockwood said. "I owe both of you my life. Thank you."

"You're welcome, sir."

Lockwood looked at Lancaster.

"I've got to get these bodies off the street," he said. "How about we meet in the saloon in half an hour and I'll buy you that beer?"

"Fine." Lancaster put his hand on Aaron's shoulder. "Maybe I'll just buy our young hero here something in the general store." He looked at the boy. "Maybe some candy?"

The boy's eyes lit up, but he said, "I'll have to ask."

"Ask who? Your father?"

"I don't have a father."

"Then who did you come to town with?"

"Mr. Bristow."

"Who's Mr. Bristow."

"He's our . . ." the boy groped for a word, "um, guide, I guess, or . . . wagon master?"

"Are you part of a wagon train?" Lockwood asked. He looked at Lancaster. "There hasn't been a wagon train through here in over twenty years."

Lancaster knew that the heyday of the wagon trains ran from 1830 to 1860, and most of that along the Oregon Trail. He also knew that jumping-off points for the trail were Missouri and Iowa—right here in Council Bluffs being one of them.

But he doubted that this boy was part of a full-fledged wagon train. With the advent of the railroad most folks chose to avoid the hardship of traveling in wagons—if they could afford it.

"Where is Mr. Bristow, son?" the sheriff asked.

Before the boy could answer a man came up behind Sheriff Lockwood.

"Sheriff?"

"Yeah, Rollins?" Lockwood asked. From the look of distaste on his face Lancaster assumed that Rollins was not one of the sheriff's favorite people.

"We got a man down in the street who wasn't part of the gang, sir." Rollins said.

"Where is he?"

"Back here, behind the buckboard."

Lockwood turned to Lancaster again, indicated his bloody side.

"We're gonna have to have the doc take a look at you."

"Let's take a look at this man first," Lancaster said. He turned to Aaron. "You better stick with us, son, until we locate your Mr. Bristow."

"Yes, sir."

They all walked over to where a man lay in the street, clutching his stomach. Blood seeped out from between the fingers.

"That's him!" Aaron shouted, pointing at the wounded man.

"That's who, Aaron?" Lancaster asked.

"That's him," the boy said, again. "That's Mr. Bristow."

"He must have been hit by a stray bullet," Lockwood said. "Rollins, let's get this man to the doctor's office."

"Yes, sir."

They lifted Bristow as gingerly as they could and then started walking toward the doctor's office, with Lancaster and Aaron following.

Chapter Six

While the doctor worked on Mr. Bristow, Lancaster talked with Aaron, trying to get more information out of the boy.

"What about your mother?" he asked.

"I don't have a mother," Aaron said. "None of us do."

"None of you? How many children are there?"

"Um, a lot. I'm not sure how many. Maybe . . . twenty?"

"Twenty kids?"

"Maybe more."

"What ages?"

The boy shrugged.

"All ages."

"Why are you all in wagons and not on a train?"

Another shrug.

"Miss Bennett said they didn't have enough money to take us all on a train."

"Who's Miss Bennett?"

"One of the ladies who takes care of us."

"So there are over twenty children and some ladies?"

Aaron nodded.

"How many ladies?"

"Four."

"And are there any men?"

Aaron nodded.

"Three."

"Including Mr. Bristow?"

"Yes."

"And who are the other two?"

"Mr. Dobbs and Mr. Will."

"And are any of these ladies and these men married?"

"No," Aaron said, "they work for us."

"So the ladies hired the men to take you all west?"

"Yes."

Lancaster wondered if he was getting the real story from the boy, or if he had a vivid imagination. Before he could ask any more questions a door opened and the sheriff stepped out. Ben Lockwood looked no worse for wear for his experience, which impressed Lancaster.

25

"How is he?" Lancaster asked.

"He wants to see you."

"Me?"

The lawman nodded.

"I'll stay with the boy."

Lancaster looked at Aaron and said, "I'll be right back."

"Okay,"

As Lancaster rose and turned his back to Aaron he blocked the boy's view of the sheriff, who took the opportunity to catch Lancaster's eye and shake his head.

Lancaster went through the door into the doctor's surgery. His nostrils were immediately assailed by the odor of death coming from the men lying on the table. The doctor turned as he entered and Lancaster saw small gray eyes peering from a heavily lined face beneath a thatch of snow white hair.

"He's asking for you," the man said.

"He doesn't even know me."

The doctor stood up and faced Lancaster.

"He saw what you did out there. He wants to ask you something."

With that the physician stepped aside so Lancaster could approach the table. The doctor had patched Bristow's belly as well as he could, but the odor of death was coming up from the wound.

"Bristow?"

26

The injured man opened his eyes and looked up at Lancaster.

"You're—you're him? The man who h-helped the sheriff?"

"That's right. My name is Lancaster."

Bristow closed his eyes. His face was deathly pale, and there was no color in his lips, either. For a moment Lancaster thought he'd passed away, but then he moistened his lips and opened his eyes.

"I don't have long," the man said. "I know that. Is—is Aaron all right?"

"He's fine," Lancaster said. "He was very brave, out there."

"He's a g—good kid."

"Yes, he is."

"Trust Aaron," Bristow said. "He'll take you to the others."

"The others? You mean— "

"Help them," Bristow said, reaching out for Lancaster's hand. The man's strength, given his condition, was amazing. "You got to help them."

"Aren't there two other men with them?"

"Don't . . . trust . . . them."

"Mr. Bristow, I—"

Lancaster knew death well. He'd dealt with it many times. Bristow's grasp on his hand went limp, and the man was dead. Just like that. He placed the hand on the man's chest and said, "Doctor?"

"Excuse me."

27

He stepped aside and let the doctor approach the table.

"He's gone. He never had a chance." He turned to look at Lancaster. "There was nothing I could do."

"I understand, Doctor," Lancaster said. "I believe he did, too."

"The boy outside is not his?"

"No," Lancaster said. "Did he tell you anything . . . helpful?"

"He didn't talk to me," the doctor said. "He told the sheriff he wanted to talk to the man who helped him. You better let me clean and bind your wound before you leave."

So the doctor had nothing to add. All Lancaster had was a few sentences from Bristow, including his last three words. "Don't trust them."

He didn't know if Bristow meant that he didn't trust the other two men, or that Lancaster shouldn't trust them.

Chapter Seven

Lancaster had not learned much more from Bristow than he had from Aaron. But he did know that there were some women and children camped somewhere out of town who probably needed help—more help, if Bristow was distrustful of the two men he'd left with them. And yet if he didn't trust them, why had he left them alone?

Instead of meeting in the saloon for a drink Lancaster took Aaron and returned to the sheriff's office with Sheriff Lockwood.

"I need a drink," Lockwood said.

He went to his desk and took out a bottle of whiskey. Lancaster could see that the man's hands were shaking. The reaction from what had almost happened was setting in.

"You mind grabbing those cups off the stove?" he asked.

Lancaster went to the pot-bellied stove and took the two tin cups from it. He handed them to Lockwood, who poured a dollop of whiskey into each and handed one back. Aaron sat in a chair against the wall and watched the two men. He had not yet been told that Mr. Bristow was dead.

"Here's to your quick actions," he said.

"And Aaron's," Lancaster added.

Both men turned and raised their cups to the boy.

"To Aaron," the lawman said.

The boy looked embarrassed. They both drained their cups. The sheriff offered Lancaster a refill, but he declined. The lawman then refilled his own cup, and put the bottle away.

"Now what?" Lockwood asked.

"I guess I'll have to take Aaron back to his people," Lancaster said, "and find out if they're all right. I'll also have to tell them about . . . about Bristow."

"Did Mr. Bristow die?" Aaron asked.

The two men exchanged a glance, and then Lancaster said, "Yes, Aaron, he did."

Aaron got off the chair, went to Lancaster and grabbed his arm.

"We have to go," he said. "We have to go and tell the others."

"Aaron," Lancaster asked, crouching down to the

boy's level, "why did you and Mr. Bristow come to town?"

"For supplies," the boy said, "and to get more help."

"More help? You mean to hire more men?"

Aaron nodded.

"Where did you all come from?"

"Philadelphia."

Coming from that far east they had been traveling for many months, already.

"And where are you heading?"

"California . . . I think."

"The only way we're going to be sure of our answers is to go out there and ask the questions," Lockwood said.

"Are you coming?"

"Why not?" the lawman asked. "I'm still the law—and I can't let you ride out there alone, not knowing what's waiting for you. I owe you—and Aaron—that much, don't I?"

Chapter Eight

Bristow had made Aaron memorize the route they'd taken to town, and the boy had done a fine job. When they came into the clearing they saw five wagons and two campfires, and around the fires were the women and children Aaron had told them about. However, nowhere to be seen were there any men or—for that matter—any horses.

They rode up to the camp and Aaron immediately dropped to the ground and ran into the arms of a blond woman, who embraced him warmly.

"Mr. Bristow's dead," he said, with his face pressed to her.

"Oh God," one of the other women said aloud, "what else can happen to us now?"

Lancaster and Sheriff Lockwood both dismounted

and approached the women and children on foot. They'd apparently been through a lot, and neither man wanted to cause them any further trepidation.

"Are you Miss Bennett?" Lancaster asked.

The woman looked up at Lancaster and, maintaining her hold on the boy, said, "Yes, Trudy Bennett. And who am I addressing?"

Lancaster paused—the woman's beauty was so great that it caused him to hesitate just a moment before replying.

"My name is Lancaster, Ma'am, and this is Sheriff Lockwood, of Council Bluffs."

"Gentlemen," she said, "thank you for bringing Aaron home safely."

"I think you have that turned around, Ma'am," the sheriff said. "Young Aaron here had a hand in saving my life, along with Mr. Lancaster."

"Really?" Trudy Bennett looked down at Aaron, who at that moment looked up at her.

"I only grabbed the horse," he told her, "to keep the sheriff from gettin' hung."

"Hung?" one of the other women echoed, and suddenly there were four women on their feet, several of them with small children clinging to them.

"And what, may I ask, happened to Mr. Bristow?" Trudy Bennett asked.

"I'm afraid he was struck by a stray bullet, Ma'am," Lancaster said. "He lingered, and then died."

"Oh God!" one of the other women wailed. "What will become of us now?"

"Hush up, Martha," Trudy Bennett said, with some iron in her tone. "Let's allow these gentlemen to tell us the whole story. I'm sorry we can't offer you any refreshment, but we are out of supplies at the moment. But perhaps you'll simply sit at our fire and explain everything?"

"Yes, Ma'am," Lancaster said. "We'd be happy to."

All the women and children in the group crowded around one fire to listen to Lancaster and Sheriff Lockwood tell their story. Lancaster saw at least twenty children ranging in age from about two or three up to twelve or thirteen. They all listened with rapt attention, eyes wide and mouths open. Some of them were reduced to tears when Lancaster told how Mr. Bristow had died, and what his last words were.

"Speaking of which," Lancaster said, looking around, "where are the two men he was talking about."

"They're gone," Trudy Bennett said.

"Where did they go?" the sheriff asked.

"We don't know," she said. "They left the night before last, and took whatever supplies we had left, and the horses."

"What?" Lockwood said. "They left you stranded?"

"Yes, sir," Trudy said, "they did. These children haven't eaten in two days."

"Well, we can fix that," Lockwood said. "I'll go to town and come back with enough food for them and for you women."

"I thought Aaron said there were four women?" Lancaster said.

"There were," Trudy said. "Well, the fourth was more child than woman, I guess. Her name is Kate, and she's eighteen."

"Where is she?" Lancaster asked.

The three women exchanged glances and then Trudy, who seemed to be in charge, said, "They took her, too."

"My God!" Lockwood said.

"Can you get her back, Sheriff?" one of the other women asked. She looked older than both Trudy and the third woman, who appeared to be in their twenties. This woman seemed to be in her forties, although all three women were showing the effects of months of travel by wagon, which probably made their ages difficult to gauge.

"I'd need a posse," Lockwood said, "and at the moment I'm not sure I could raise one. Council Bluffs is going through a kind of . . . crisis, at the moment."

"We need our horses," Trudy said, which Lancaster found odd. She seemed more concerned about the horses than the young woman. "We can't afford to buy more, and we're not going anywhere without them."

"We could settle here," the third woman said.

"This was not our goal, Donna," Trudy said.

"It doesn't look like we're going to reach our goal, Trudy," the older woman said.

"Martha," Trudy said, "we can't give up. We've been through too much already." She looked at Lancaster. "We've had three children die since we left Philadelphia."

Sheriff Lockwood stood up.

"I think the important thing at the moment is to get these children fed," he said.

Lancaster remained seated, looked up at the lawman. He felt the sheriff still needed a day or two to recover from his recent ordeal. Perhaps feeding the children was as much as he'd be able to handle. That meant that the job of getting the horses—and Kate—back was going to fall to him by default.

He stood up, excused himself, and pulled the sheriff aside to discuss it with him.

Chapter Nine

Things had been happening fast since Lancaster arrived in Council Bluffs—and even before that. Both he and Sheriff Lockwood needed some time to recover, so they agreed that the lawman would ride back to town and return with some food, while Lancaster would stay with the women and children.

"The town didn't exactly come to your rescue, Sheriff," Lancaster commented. "Are you sure they'll come to the aid of this group?"

"Going up against an outlaw gang and getting killed is one thing," Lockwood said. "Letting a group of children starve is another one, entirely."

"I have to say you're a very understanding man."

"Almost getting hanged was part of my job, Lancaster," Lockwood said. "So is helping these people.

But don't get me wrong, I'm angry about what happened, I just haven't had the time to sit and consider it."

"Riding back to town alone might give you the time."

"What about you?" Lockwood asked. "You came to town for a beer, and so far you've been involved in a shootout, and now this. You gonna try to track these fellas down?"

"If I do it won't be until tomorrow morning," Lancaster said. "I think I also need to take some time to consider my next move."

"Taking the time to do some thinking wouldn't hurt either one of us," the lawman said.

While Lockwood headed back to town Lancaster walked back to the fire. The women and children had spread out, Aaron was seated at the fire next to Trudy, who had her arm around him. Lancaster collected some things from his saddlebags and went to join them.

"Aaron," he said, "why don't you take this beef jerky, break it up and pass it out to the children. Maybe it'll hold them until the sheriff comes back with some hot food."

Aaron looked at Trudy, who said, "It's all right, Aaron. Go ahead."

Eagerly, Aaron grabbed the food from Lancaster and ran to share with the other children.

"He's a brave little boy," Lancaster said.

"And smart. Did he . . . see Mr. Bristow die?"

"He saw a lot of things, Miss Bennett," Lancaster said. "I'm afraid Bristow, Aaron and I all rode into a bad situation."

"But you got involved," she said. "Why was that?"

"I couldn't stand by and watch the sheriff be lynched."

"Anymore than you can stand by and watch these children starve?" she asked.

"That's right. Look, I have some coffee. Why don't I make some for you and the other ladies?"

"Only if you'll join us," she said.

He smiled. "You've got a deal."

When the coffee was made Trudy took cups to Donna and Martha, then came back and drank hers with Lancaster.

"So tell me about this whole ordeal," Lancaster said.

"Why not?" Trudy said. "It wouldn't hurt for you to understand why we're doing this. Martha, Donna and I operated an orphanage in Philadelphia. Kate had been one of the children until she turned eighteen, and then she became a helper. We weren't funded, though, and depended solely on donations, which were often not very forthcoming. Well, Donna read this article about miners in California who are too busy to have families. We decided to pack up the children and take them to California to place them with some miners and their wives."

"What about the three—or four—of you?"

Now Trudy seemed to become embarrassed.

"Well, some of the miners were even looking for wives," she said.

"I see."

"We didn't have money to book passage for all of us on a train, but we didn't want to let that stop us. So we begged for supplies, and one local man said he'd provide wagons for us, and another horses."

Lancaster looked at the wagons. There were five, from what he could see, but three of them were little more than buckboards with tarps covering them, while the other two were Conestogas that had seen better days. Maybe that wasn't fair, they had probably all been in better shape when they left Philadelphia.

"But you could travel alone, just the women and children."

"No," she said, "that's where Mr. Bristow came in. He came to us one day, said he'd heard that we were going to come west. He offered his services as a sort of wagon master and guide." Those had been the two terms Aaron had used to describe the man.

"He didn't want payment?"

"He said he was originally from the west and wanted to return," she explained. "All he asked was that he be able to share in our supplies, and our company. We were happy to accept him. Along the way he and Martha started to get along very well. I—I thought they might end up together when we reached California. She's very upset about his death."

"I can understand that. But what about these other men?"

"They are not the men we left Philadelphia with," she said. "Mr. Bristow supplied us with several men to drive the wagon, but we lost them along the way. One died as the result of an accident, another decided to leave us when we were in Ohio. By the time we reached St. Louis we only had Mr. Bristow, and we were all driving wagons ourselves."

"And in St. Louis you hired these other men?"

"We had a little bit of money, Mr. Lancaster, and both Mr. Will and Mr. Dobbs seemed willing to take fifty dollars each to drive us at least this far. Upon arrival here we expected to discuss the matter further with them."

"But it didn't happen that way, did it?"

"I'm afraid not." Trudy rubbed her arms, chilled despite the warmth of the summer evening. "Not long after Mr. Bristow left for town with Aaron, Mr. Will and Mr. Dobbs became abusive. They started to remove what supplies we had left, and round the horses up together. They had saddles in one of the wagons, and put them on two of the horses. Then they took everything they could carry—including

41

Kate—and left with the horses, which they expected to be able to sell." She shrugged helplessly. "We had no way to stop them except to plead with them, but that was useless."

"You don't have any weapons?"

She bit her lip before answering. "I have several weapons hidden—a handgun, and two rifles—but none of us could have used them against Mr. Will and Mr. Dobbs without someone being hurt—perhaps some of the children." She looked away. "I felt like a coward, but—"

"Nonsense," Lancaster said, cutting her off. "You did the right thing, Miss Bennett. If you had tried to brace those men with guns, you probably would have been killed."

"I suppose." She looked at him. "You're very kind. Please, call me Trudy."

"I'm just . . . Lancaster."

"Just one name?"

"It's all I use."

She shook her head and said, "I find the men in the west very strange, indeed."

"Not all in a bad way, I hope," he said.

"Of course not," she said. "How could I ever think badly of you? Look at what you've done."

If she only knew what he'd done in the past, before Becky Pickens, the ghost with blue eyes who almost drove him crazy, and Alicia Adams, the little girl who brought him back from the brink of not only madness but self-destruction as well.

What would Trudy Bennett think of him if she knew all of that, he wondered?

Chapter Ten

When Sheriff Lockwood returned it was with a wagon loaded with supplies, and with several women from town. All of the women seemed to immediately bond and before long there was food cooking over all the fires, the children crowded excitedly around, waiting. There were no other men with Lockwood. He and Lancaster stood off to one side, drinking coffee and watching.

"The women thought the behavior of their men during a time of crisis was disgraceful," Lockwood told Lancaster. "At least, that's what they said."

"There were women at the lynching, Sheriff."

"I know that." Lockwood tossed the remnants of his coffee onto the ground. "What I don't understand is . . . Council Bluffs is growing. This is not the old west anymore. But this incident . . . it seems to have thrown this town and these people . . . I don't know, back twenty or thirty years. Why was it so easy for three men to control an entire town?"

"I don't know the answer to that," Lancaster said. "I only know that a lynch mob mentality doesn't know anything about time or place."

"Okay, but a lynch mob mentality . . . you're not talking about a town being willing to watch their sheriff be hanged. This was . . . I can't get my mind around this, Lancaster."

"Inexplicable," Lancaster said.

"What?"

"That's the word you're looking for to describe the situation."

"If you say so," the lawman said. "I don't even think I know what that means."

"It means you can't explain it. Look, you can put up modern lights or maybe start calling the local law "police" instead of sheriff or marshal, but that doesn't mean the people are going to change. You need to have some leaders in town, and it seems to me what you've got here are a bunch of followers."

"You're saying that with some more . . . responsible people involved this wouldn't have happened?"

"Look at your mayor," Lancaster said. "Sure, he was ashamed of what he was doing, but he did it."

"Fred Hansen is a coward."

"Then he shouldn't be mayor. Maybe that's your first step."

Lockwood looked away.

"Don't know if it's my first step."

"What do you mean?"

"I may not be staying on."

"Well, I couldn't blame you for that, either," Lancaster said. "I don't know that I'd stay on in a town that almost lynched me."

"It wasn't the whole town, really."

"Just a good portion of it, plus the people who run it," Lancaster pointed out. "How many members of the town council were out there watching you get lynched?"

"Most of 'em, I guess."

"The bartender, the one who got me to wear your badge," Lancaster said, "at least he took the initiative, and got something done. Maybe he should be mayor."

"Maybe. . . ."

Lancaster clapped a hand on the sheriff's shoulder and said, "Don't think I can help you with this decision, Sheriff."

The man looked at Lancaster and said, "Ben, the name's Ben."

"All right, Ben, maybe we should help the women distribute the food to the children."

"Sure. . . ."

* * *

Later, Lancaster found himself sitting next to Trudy Bennett, who had waited until everyone else was fed before she sat down to eat.

"We haven't eaten this well in quite a while," she confided to Lancaster.

He looked down at his own plate, which was filled mostly with vegetables and beans. The women from town had also brought them some canned fruit, flour and wheat, as well as coffee, all of which was loaded into one of the wagons.

"I can't tell you how much we appreciate your help, Mr. Lancaster."

"No 'Mister,' " he said. "Just Lancaster."

"Are you still going to go after our horses in the morning? And Kate?" she asked. "It would seem to me to be the sheriff's job, not yours."

"Well," Lancaster said, "the sheriff seems to be having a crisis of his own, at the moment."

"I don't wonder," she said. "Why would he want to stay on in a town that almost hung him?"

"That's what he's trying to decide, right now."

"And why would you want to get involved?"

"From the time I first rode into town it doesn't seem I've had a choice," he said. "Everything has happened too quickly. And if I don't go after your horses and the men who took them—and Kate—who will?"

"You're a very decent man," she said, "very kind—"

47

"Trudy," he said, stopping her.

"Yes?"

He wondered if he should tell her that he wasn't kind or decent—or, at least, he hadn't been for a good part of his life. But they'd just met, and he didn't feel like confiding in a perfect stranger, at the moment.

"You and the kids needs help," he said. "Why don't we just leave it at that, for now?"

Chapter Eleven

Horses were something the town wasn't ready to donate to the party of women and children, and even if they did there was still the young girl, Kate, to consider.

By the time the townswomen left, the children were well fed and sleepy. They'd been exhausted from all the travel when they had reached this point, and now just sitting around and waiting for a few days seemed to have tired them out even more. It was just starting to get dark when most of them—the youngest ones—fell asleep.

"What are you going to do?" Lockwood asked Lancaster. They were standing by their horses, which were both still saddled.

They were near one fire while the three women

and some of the older children were seated around another. Trudy seemed to be holding court there, telling them all what had happened, what was going to happen, or maybe they were discussing what should happen.

"We can't just leave these people out here alone," said Lancaster.

"We can't take them all to town," Lockwood said. "Things there are far from back to normal. I was lucky to get some of the merchants to donate food and blankets and stuff. I think they did it mostly from guilt, probably the same reason some of the women came out here with me."

"No, town is not the place for them, either," Lancaster said.

"What if they decide to stay—"

"I don't think that's going to be the case," Lancaster said, cutting him off. "Trudy's pretty determined to move on."

"So you're going to go out and find the horses, and the other girl? And brace those men?"

"There's only two of them."

"Still . . . I should go with you."

Lancaster looked at him.

"You don't owe me anything, Sheriff."

"Just my life."

"Look, you're in no condition to go man hunting," Lancaster said, "not after what happened to you, and what almost happened to you."

50

"Why should you go?"

Lancaster hesitated, then said, "That poor bastard Bristow, he asked for me. He wanted me to help these people, because he knew he was dying."

"So you're going to grant his dying wish?"

"Somebody should, don't you think?" Lancaster asked. "He didn't ask to get shot, did he?"

"Well, it wasn't your fault."

"I could have walked away," Lancaster said. "I could have mounted up and rode out of town."

"I'd be dead, then."

"And Quitman and his boys would be controlling Council Bluffs, at least for a while," Lancaster went on. "But Bristow would be alive, these people would be on their way, and—"

"You don't know any of that," the lawman said. "The other two, Will and Dobbs, would still have run off. These people would still be stranded, and neither you nor I would be here to help them—and if Quitman was running the town, do you think he would?"

"Okay," Lancaster said, "so we can't play 'if' or 'maybe.' We can only go along with what is happening now. You have to recover from what happened and make up your mind as to what you're going to do with your own life. Me, I'll just have to follow through with what I started."

"You know," Lockwood said, "your name has been familiar to me ever since I first heard it."

"Is that right?"

"You really handled yourself out there today," the other man said. "Like . . . like it was your business to do that."

Lancaster didn't reply.

"Oh, don't worry," Lockwood said. "I'm not gonna go back to town and check wanted posters or anything. I still owe you my life."

Lancaster still didn't offer anything.

"So, what *are* you gonna do?"

"I'll spend the night here, and in the morning I'll start tracking. They have a head start but they're leaving a hell of a trail with ten horses."

"If I had any deputies I could rely on . . ."

"Don't worry about it," Lancaster said. "You were right about one thing. This is what I do best. And there *are* only two of them."

The two men shook hands, and as the sheriff rode off Lancaster started unsaddling his horse.

Chapter Twelve

Lancaster put on another pot of coffee. It was quiet, as everyone was asleep by now. He looked up at the almost full moon, wondering whether he could have tracked by moonlight. He heard someone moving around and then saw Aaron approaching the fire.

"Can't sleep?"

The boy rubbed his eyes. "I had a dream about Mr. Bristow. Can I sit with you for a while?"

"Sure," Lancaster said. "Pull up a rock."

Aaron sat next to him and stared into the fire. Lancaster thought about telling him not to, but he didn't know if the boy would need to know about night vision when he grew up. Trudy had said he was smart. Maybe he'd end up working in a city like San Francisco or Denver, and would never need to know how staring into a fire destroyed your night vision.

"You don't drink coffee, do you?"

"No, sir."

"How about some water?"

"Yes."

Lancaster passed Aaron his canteen. The boy took two swallows and passed it back.

"Are you going after Mr. Will and Mr. Dobbs tomorrow?"

"Yes, I am."

"To get back the horses?"

"And Kate," Lancaster said. "You want me to bring back Kate, don't you?"

Aaron shrugged.

"Are you going to kill them?"

"I hope not," Lancaster said. "I just want to bring back Kate and the horses so you can all be on your way again."

"We can't go alone."

"You're not alone," Lancaster said. "You'll all be together."

"No," Aaron said, "I mean without you."

"Me? I can't go with you."

Aaron scratched his nose and said, "But you have to."

"Why do I have to, Aaron?"

"Because Mr. Bristow is dead," the boy said. "We need someone to take us."

"Aaron," Lancaster said, "I'm going to help get your horses back, but I have my own life. I can't just take Mr. Bristow's place."

"But he wanted you to help," Aaron said, "to take care of us. He asked you. I heard you say so."

"Aaron . . . maybe you should try to get back to sleep now," Lancaster suggested.

"You don't want to talk to me, anymore," the boy said, astutely.

"Aaron—"

"It's okay, I understand." Aaron stood up. "But you have to think about it. Okay?"

"Uh, okay."

Aaron nodded, as if his goal had been achieved, and returned to the wagon he'd been sleeping underneath. The smaller children were asleep inside of the wagons.

"I told you he was smart," Trudy said, from behind him.

He turned his head and looked at her over his shoulder.

"You knew I was here, listening?" she asked.

"I knew somebody was there," he said. "Coffee?"

"Thank you."

She came and sat down next to him, the same place Aaron had been, and accepted the cup from him.

"I heard what Aaron said to you," she commented. "It wasn't really fair."

He nodded, sipped his own coffee.

"You've done enough already," she went on, "and tomorrow you're going after Mr. Will and Mr. Dobbs. What more could we expect of you?"

Lancaster wondered if he was being played, first by Aaron, and now by Trudy. Maybe they were working as a team to get him to take them to California.

"There might be someone in town willing to take you," he said. "Depending on how much you can pay."

"It's not how much we can pay," she said, "but if we can pay. We had to give Mr. Bristow his money in advance."

"And the other two?"

"We were supposed to pay them when we arrived," she said, "or when we parted company. We gave them something in advance, but not much."

"With everything else that they stole did they take whatever money you do have?"

"No," she said, "I have that money hidden . . . but it isn't much. In fact, Mr. Bristow had some of that money on him, to buy supplies. Do you think we can get it back?"

"Sure," Lancaster said, "or the supplies. Either one."

"Good," she said. "I'd just hate to lose that money."

Lancaster poured himself some more coffee.

"Trudy," he said, "I would like to help you, I would. I'd like to take you to California—"

"Oh, we couldn't pay you—"

"I've done a lot in my life I need to atone for," he said, cutting her off. "Taking you and the children and the other women to California would help me to do that."

"What could you possibly have done to atone for?" she asked, innocently.

Lancaster took a moment, then said, "Let's not get into that now. I think I need to get some sleep if I'm going to catch up to Dobbs and Will and get your horses back for you."

"All right." She handed him the cup back. "Good night. I'll see you in the morning."

"Good night, Trudy."

Lancaster decided to roll himself up in his bedroll before somebody else came along for a little chat.

Chapter Thirteen

The women from town had brought enough supplies so that Lancaster woke to the smell of flapjacks. He rolled out of his bedroll and checked his gun first thing. This was a habit he had fallen into very early in life, which was the reason he was alive, healthy and approaching middle age.

When he was sure his weapon was in working order he approached one of the fires.

"Coffee, Mr. Lancaster?" Martha asked.

"Yes, thank you."

She handed him a steaming cup and said, "I'm preparing another batch of flapjacks. Should be ready any minute." She looked around at the children of varying ages, who had one thing in common—they were devouring their breakfast.

"It's been so long since they had a breakfast like this," she told Lancaster. "They have been so well behaved and brave on this journey, they deserve this."

"Well, make sure they're all fed before you give me a plate," he told her.

"Well, as I understand it," she said, "you're going to go out looking for Kate and our horses this morning, so you're going to need all your strength. I'll be getting you a plate very soon."

"All right," he said, rather than argue with her.

He stood there drinking his coffee and gradually became aware of the fact that he was the center of attention. He looked down at the children who, while still eating, raised their eyes to study him. Some seemed in awe of his height, others just seemed curious about him. Or maybe they were looking at him the way some people would look at a priest—or a savior.

That was it. Word had gotten around that he was going to help them, maybe even take them to California. Perhaps they'd even heard about what he'd done in town.

"Here you go, Mr. Lancaster," Martha said, handing him a heaping helping of flapjacks.

"Thank you, Ma'am."

"Oh, you can just call me Martha," she said. "Everybody else does."

"All right, Martha," he said, "and you can just

59

call me Lancaster. There's no need for a 'Mister' in front of it."

"Whatever you say," she responded, and then he realized she was looking at him the same way.

"I'm just going to walk over here and eat," he said, pointing away from the fire. "I seem to be distracting the children from their meal."

"It's just that they've never seen a man like you before."

He decided not to ask what she meant by that. He simply put some distance between himself and the children before he started to eat.

Before long Trudy came walking over to him with a coffee pot in her hands.

"A refill?"

"Thank you, and good morning," he said, holding out the cup. "I'll have one more and then I'll have to be on my way." As she filled his cup he asked, "When exactly did Will and Dobbs leave camp, Trudy?"

"Well, Mr. Bristow and Aaron left early yesterday morning. Those men must have planned to leave us stranded the first chance they got. They didn't wait very long after that to start unhitching the horses and stealing our supplies."

"What about Kate, Trudy?"

"What about her?"

"How did they decide to take her with them?"

"Kate's a very pretty girl, and both Mr. Will and

Mr. Dobbs are in their early thirties. They had obviously decided long ago that they were going to take her, too."

"Did they make any advances . . . I mean, did they try to take any of the other women?" Lancaster asked. "You, or Martha, or—"

"Heavens, no." Trudy said. "As I said, they must have made their choice long ago. Kate was the youngest woman, and the prettiest."

"Well," Lancaster said, "I think you're being a bit modest."

"I'm sorry?" she asked.

He stared at her for a moment, then realized that she truly did not understand what he was referring to. Could she have been unaware of her own beauty?

"I'm sure she can't be that much prettier than you."

She touched her face and looked away.

"We've been traveling quite a long time, Lancaster," she said. "I'm afraid the sun and the dust take their toll on everyone but the young."

"Oh, I don't know," he said. "Some of these kids look pretty worn out."

"Well," Trudy said, "for some reason the trip did not seem to be having that effect on Kate."

Lancaster decided not to argue the point with her. It had very little to do with what was going on.

"Is the sheriff coming back this morning?" she asked.

"I don't know," Lancaster said. "He'll probably be bringing back either your supplies or whatever money Bristow was carrying. If he does it will be after I leave."

"When will that be?"

"As soon as I finish these flapjacks," he said. "I hope the kids don't get used to this kind of breakfast."

"This was a special occasion," she said. "We'll go back to rationing food after this."

Lancaster finished off his breakfast and gave Trudy the plate and cup to return to Martha. She came up behind him while he was saddling his horse.

"I want you to know how much we appreciate this," she said, "but we don't want you to die for us."

"I don't intend to die." He cinched his saddle tightly and then turned to face her. "Trudy, I need you to tell me something about these two men I'm tracking."

"What can I tell you?"

"What were they like? Did they seem competent to you? What about their guns?"

"They had pistols and rifles, but I really don't know much about guns—or western men, for that matter."

"You have to give me something," he said. "Did they treat their weapons well? Clean them? Play with them?"

"Play with them?"

"Did they shoot at tin cans? Twirl their guns? Leave them holstered or take them out a lot?"

"Oh, I see. Mr. Will liked to take his gun out and show it to the children. He did twirl it quite a bit. As for Mr. Dobbs, he spent a lot of time cleaning his rifle."

"Okay, that helps."

"In what way?"

"Dobbs sounds like a man who is serious about his weapons, and Will sounds like a man who has an exaggerated idea of his own ability with a gun. A show-off. That helps me to decide which of them will be more dangerous when the time comes. What do they look like?"

Trudy described Will as tall, rangy, and said she was surprised at how small his hands were. Dobbs, she said, was not as tall, but was wider, with thick-fingered hands. Her description of Dobbs' hands told Lancaster why the man spent more time on his rifle than his handgun. She had previously said both were in their thirties.

"Did either of them try to show off any sort of physical prowess other than Will's twirling of his gun?"

"No," she said, "but I did notice how strong Mr.

Will was when the wheel on one of the wagons broke. He actually lifted the wagon."

"With no help?'

"Not from either of the other men, but he did use a rather large tree branch."

Even using the branch for leverage it was quite a feat for one man to lift a wagon off the ground. Will sounded like the more dangerous of the two men.

"All right," he said, "see, you were more helpful than you thought you could be."

He turned and mounted up, then looked down at her. Before he could leave the other women came over with some of the kids, and Aaron came close to the horse.

"Mr. Lancaster, you're not gonna get killed like Mr. Bristow, are you?" the boy asked.

"No, Aaron," he said, "I'm not going to get killed."

"Promise?"

"I promise."

He hoped it was a promise he was going to keep.

Chapter Fourteen

Frank Will looked across the fire at Ted Dobbs, who was very busily eating his eggs. Will never knew how Dobbs could concentrate that hard on one thing. He was always thinking about many things at once.

"Did you hear me?" he asked.

Dobbs raised his eyes from his plate.

"What?"

"I asked you how long we're gonna keep this girl with us?"

Dobbs waited to reply until he had shoveled the last of his eggs into his mouth, and then washed it down with the last of his coffee.

"You gonna make breakfast like this every morning?" he asked.

"Wha—no. You know I can't cook. You been doin' the cookin' for us for years."

"Exactly. So now she cooks, and it's good."

Will waited, then said, "So? How long?"

Dobbs refilled his own cup and said, "As long as we got food to cook."

"Ted," Will said, "don't you think somebody is gonna come lookin' for her?"

"Like who?" Dobbs asked.

"Well, Bristow, for one."

"He wouldn't leave the rest of them to come after this one," Dobbs said. "He's too responsible for that."

"Then maybe he'll go to the law."

"By the time some lawdog gets on our trail we'll be long gone," Dobbs said. "You know how long it takes to get a posse together? There ever been a posse we couldn't outrun?"

"Well, no—"

"And there ain't never gonna be," Dobbs said. "Come on, man, taste this coffee. You ever have coffee this good on the trail before?"

Actually, Will didn't even like coffee all that much, so he didn't know good from bad.

"Well, what about these horses?" he asked. "When we gonna sell 'em?"

"Let's put some good distance between us and Council Bluffs before we try to sell 'em."

"We're low on money, ya know," Will said.

"They didn't have any hid away like you thought."

"Well then, they're damned fools to leave Philadelphia without some cash in reserve," Dobbs said.

"I thought they was crazy from the beginning, traveling all that way with a bunch of kids."

"Yeah, well . . ." he looked around. "Where is the girl, anyway?"

"Down by the stream washing our clothes."

"See?" Dobbs said. "One of us would be doin' that if she wasn't here."

"Then what about . . . other needs."

"Like what?"

"You know what I'm talkin' about, Ted," Will said.

Dobbs stared at Will, who was never sure when his partner was funning with him because he did it so infrequently.

"Do you mean you want to start treatin' her less like a lady?" Dobbs asked.

"I mean we been travelin' with a bunch of women for a while, most of them I wouldn't'a minded treatin' like less of a lady," Will said, "but this one is askin' for it. Twitchin' her butt around us like she is, she's just askin' for it."

"Well, I guess we'll see," Ted Dobbs said. "Why don't you check on the horses, make sure they're all tied off good and tight. We don't need any of them gettin' away."

"Buncha nags, if you ask me," Will said, standing

and wiping his hands off on his thighs. "Probably won't get all that much more 'em, anyway."

"Like you said, Frank," Dobbs replied, "we're runnin' low on cash, so whatever we get will be more than we got now."

As Will walked toward the horses Dobbs stood up, wiped off his own hands, and started toward the stream.

Chapter Fifteen

The trail was as plain as day to follow, as Lancaster had assumed it would be. You can't drive ten horses and not leave a sign behind. He was not the world's greatest tracker, but even he could follow this trail.

Also, they were not going fast. They had a full day's head start on him, but they probably didn't think anyone was coming after them—or, if someone was, that they would not have gotten started as quickly as Lancaster had. Traveling alone as he was, his travel time could be two or three times theirs. At that rate he could catch up to them in, perhaps, half a day—twelve hours. But that would mean traveling for that entire twelve hours without stopping, and he knew that he and his horse would need rest sometime. Better to figure tracking them for a full day, and catching up to them sometime tomorrow.

And once he caught them, then what? Bring the horses and the girl back to the group, tip his hat and say adios? He knew that wasn't going to happen. Unless he could find someone in Council Bluffs willing to lead them to California for little or no money, he was going to end up doing it. He knew that. There were too many kids involved—in particular, Aaron. The boy looked at him with big, round eyes, and ever since Alicia Adams he found it very hard to resist a personable, intelligent child when they were in need.

And that was not to mention the women who were in need. He tried not to think about Trudy Bennett as anything but a woman toting a wagonload of trouble, but he couldn't do it. She was just too damned pretty.

Kids and women. They were an unbeatable combination when they were in trouble.

Aaron stayed by Trudy's side for most of the morning after Lancaster rode off, and she finally crouched down and asked the boy what was bothering him.

"I'm afraid Mr. Lancaster is gonna get killed."

"Why is that, Aaron? He seems very capable to me. Why, you saw what he did when he saved the sheriff?"

"Yes," Aaron said, "but he needed *my* help, and I'm not with him to help him now."

"Well, that's true," she said, "but that's because you have to be here to help me. We have to get the other children, and the wagons, ready to travel again."

"We're not gonna stay here?"

"No," she said, shaking her head. "We can't stay here. We have people waiting for us in California, don't we?"

"Yes, Ma'am."

She stood up then, and he peered up at her, closing one eye against the sun that was behind her.

"Is there something else, Aaron?"

"Do you like Mr. Lancaster?"

"Well . . . I don't know him very well, do I?" she asked. "I—I suppose I like him just fine."

She wondered why the question made her so uncomfortable?

"He likes you."

"Really? Did he say so?"

"I can tell."

"I think perhaps we'd better get back to work, Aaron," she said. "When Mr. Lancaster returns with the horses we have to be ready to hitch them up and be on our way."

"Who's gonna drive the wagons?"

He was a perceptive boy. They had five wagons, and even if Kate returned with Lancaster they only had four women—and Kate was rather useless when it came to any kind of hard work.

"Well, that's just something we're going to have to decide later, Aaron," she said, "when the time comes."

"Yes, Ma'am."

"Come on," she said, making a shooing motion at him, "let's get back to work."

Later in the afternoon Sheriff Lockwood did finally return. He was driving a wagon, this time, rather than riding a horse, and the wagon had supplies in it—although it was not heavily laden with them.

"Good afternoon, Sheriff," Trudy said, when the man stepped down.

"Ma'am," he said. He gave the camp a brief once-over. "Has Lancaster gone, then?"

"He rode out this morning," she said. "He seemed to think he could track down Mr. Will and Mr. Dobbs without any problem."

"Tracking them's one thing," he said, "bringing them back is another."

"Do you suppose he intends to bring them back?"

The man stared at her for a moment, then said, "I don't rightly know, Ma'am. He's sure capable of killing them if they resist."

Trudy Bennett didn't want to talk about killing, so she changed the subject.

"What's in the wagon?"

"These are supplies your Mr. Bristow had bought and paid for before the commotion in town," the sheriff said. "I thought I'd bring them out to you."

"That's very kind of you. Thank you."

Although the wagon was not completely filled with supplies, she could see that there were more there than Bristow would have been able to afford. It seemed to Trudy that the people of Council Bluffs were not done with their giving.

"I'll just unload them for you," Lockwood said.

"Thank you, Sheriff."

She folded her arms as he went to work, and couldn't help thinking about Lancaster, at that moment. Would he end up killing two men because of them? She shuddered to think so, but shivered even more at the alternative.

Chapter Sixteen

The thing Lancaster had in his favor was that the extra horses Will and Dobbs had were not saddle mounts. If they had been they could have used them as relief mounts, and he'd never catch up to them. But having to lead the ten of them was definitely going to slow them down.

As the day went on he could see the trail getting more and more fresh. That night he made a cold camp, and when he rose in the morning he breakfasted on beef jerky and got right back on the trail. Before long he came upon the campfire they'd made the night before and it was still warm. He was only hours behind them, now. With a little luck he'd have them in sight before they camped for the night. That would give him time to plan his move.

* * *

"Goddamn nags!" Frank Will cursed.

Dobbs and Kate were riding ahead while Will drove the horses from behind. Despite the dust the horses were kicking up in his face he could see Kate's blond hair shining in the sun ahead of him. He resented having to ride drag while Dobbs got to ride with the girl.

He was also supposed to be watching their back trail, but was more interested in what was ahead of him.

The dust was the tip-off that he had finally caught up to them. Will, Dobbs and Bristow had had their own saddle horses, so there were thirteen animals up there ahead of him kicking up some dust.

And then as he topped a rise there they were, just ahead of him. There was one man behind the ten horses, and ahead of them the other man and the girl. Obviously, Kate must have been riding Bristow's horse, and he could plainly see the sun shining on her blond hair.

Lancaster backed off, then, because if the man riding drag turned in his saddle to look behind them he'd have spotted him. He didn't need to keep them in sight to follow them. The dust was enough. Now all he had to do was wait for them to camp for the night.

* * *

"Take care of the horses," Dobbs told Will.

"And what are you gonna do?"

"I'm gonna build the fire."

"And take care of the girl, right? You get to ride next to her all day and then take care of her at night?"

"Frank, do you want to build the fire?"

"Yeah," Will said, "yeah, I'll build the fire, and you take care of the horses. How about that?"

"That's fine," Dobbs said. "I don't have a problem with that."

"Good."

Dobbs turned and called out to Kate.

"Come on," he said, "help me secure the horses."

He took her hand and walked her away from Will, who stared after them with his mouth open.

Lancaster left his horse a hundred yards back and, after securing his mount, made his way toward the camp on foot. There was still a half hour's worth of daylight and he was trying to decide whether to make his move now or wait for darkness. He watched as Dobbs and Kate made sure all of the horses were secure. They tied a rope off between two trees and then tied the horses off to that line. Meanwhile, in camp Frank Will was stomping around, building the fire and muttering to himself.

Trudy Bennett had done a good job of describing the two men and they were easy to tell apart.

Lancaster had his rifle and was on higher ground. He could have pinned them down from there, but there was always the chance they'd take refuge behind Kate, using her as a hostage.

He decided that the best thing to do was to get closer, and for that he'd have to wait until after nightfall. He settled down on his belly to watch and wait.

Will was still fuming as Kate—crouching over the fire, humming—cooked up a mess of bacon and beans. Every once in a while she threw a look Dobbs' way—the kind of look Will wished she would give him.

"Kate," Dobbs said, when he and Will each had a plate, "before you start to eat there's a bottle of whiskey in my saddlebags. Fetch it for me, will you?"

"Sure, Ted."

As Kate ran off toward Dobbs' horse Will leaned across the fire and hissed, "You had her already, didn't you?"

"Don't be silly," Dobbs said. "When did I have time to have her without you knowing?"

"I don't know," the other man said, sourly, "but

you did. I can see the way she's lookin' at you."

"You're crazy, Frank."

"I ain't crazy," Will said, "don't say that, Ted—"

"Frank take it easy—"

"Both of you stand fast!" another man's voice called out, and both men froze.

Chapter Seventeen

Lancaster crept down close to the camp as night fell, remained outside the circle of light given off by the campfire and waited his chance. When he saw Kate move away from the two men he seized his chance. He rose, rifle ready, advanced into the camp and shouted, "Both of you stand fast!"

The two men looked like they were starting an argument, but at the sound of his voice they froze. He moved into the light, holding his rifle on them.

"Who the hell are you?" Dobbs demanded.

"The name's Lancaster. I'm here for those horses, and the girl."

"Get your own," Will said.

"Oh, I know these aren't mine," Lancaster said, "but I also know they're not yours. And I know who you stole them from. My plan is to return them."

"Bristow sent you?" Dobbs asked. "Wasn't he man enough to come himself?"

"Bristow's dead," Lancaster said. "Caught a stray bullet while he was in town."

"Ain't that too bad," Will said.

Both men stood, remaining on either side of the fire.

"Go easy, boys," Lancaster said. "I just want the girl and the horses and whatever else you stole from those nice people."

"Stupid people, you mean" Will said. "They ain't never gonna make it to California in one piece. If it wasn't us takin' everythin' from them it woulda been somebody else. Tell you what, we'll split everything with you. How's that? Take five horses."

"And who gets the girl?" Lancaster asked.

"I do," Dobbs said, and suddenly he went for his gun.

The move surprised Lancaster, but he was ready for it. He pulled the trigger on his rifle, but Dobbs was moving as he fired. Lancaster's bullet struck him, but it hit him in the side and not in anything vital. The man grunted, threw himself to the ground and fired his own weapon. His hasty shot missed, but Lancaster had to duck and then Will was moving, too. Lancaster went to one knee and fired at him. Will was not as lucky as Dobbs, nor as fast with his gun. He barely had it clear of leather before Lancaster put a bullet in his chest.

He didn't wait to see Will fall. He rolled just as Dobbs came up on one knee and fired again. Lancaster rolled twice, came to a stop and fired. This time his shot was true, and lethal. It struck Dobbs in the forehead, snapping his head back. He remained like that for a moment, suspended, his body undecided which way it was going to fall, and then he went down face first into the fire.

Lancaster rose, rushed to the body and pulled it clear of the fire. The man's face was badly burned, but he was beyond feeling it. Will was dead, too, but Lancaster took the time to kick his gun into the darkness, anyway.

Suddenly, he heard someone screaming and when he turned he saw the girl charging at him, hands raised. He dropped his rifle and caught her as she struck his chest. Her weight took him down onto his back and he fought her as she tried to first hit him, and then scratch his eyes out.

"Kate take it easy!" he shouted. "I'm not going to hurt you. Trudy sent me."

But she continued to scream and claw at him, until finally he rolled her over and pinned her hands to the ground.

"I said take it easy," he yelled. "I'm here to take you back!"

"You bastard!" she shouted, her faced contorted and ugly. "I don't want to go back."

Stunned, he released his hold on her wrists and stood up. She remained on the ground and he stared down at her.

"What are you talking about?" he asked. "These men kidnapped you against your will and you don't—"

He stopped as she started to laugh. He looked around the camp, even though he knew no one else was watching this. He thought maybe the girl had gone crazy. Perhaps they'd raped her, and driven her out of her mind.

"I don't get it," he said finally.

She got to her feet and brushed the dirt from her dress.

"They didn't kidnap me, you idiot," she said. "I asked them to take me with them."

"But . . . why?"

"Because I wanted to get away," she said. "Away from those women, and those kids. They were driving me crazy. When Dobbs and Will said they were taking everything and leaving, I begged them to take me with them."

Lancaster was confused. No one had told him this.

"They didn't tell you, did they?" she asked, as if reading his mind. "They didn't tell you that I went willingly?"

"No, they didn't."

"Typical."

She looked down at the two dead men.

"Well, we've got two choices then," she said. "You can take me back, because I'm not staying out here alone."

"Or?"

She smiled what was probably meant to be a seductive smile, and said, "You and me can go on. We can find somebody to buy these horses and then keep going. . . ." She stopped because she could see that he wasn't interested.

Lancaster did not think of Kate as a woman, but as a child, and he found nothing in her demeanor to be seductive or tempting. To him, she was no match for the beauty and class of a Trudy Bennett.

"We're going back, then?" she asked.

He nodded.

"We're going back."

She sighed and looked around again.

"Well, you get these bodies out of here and I'll see what I can salvage for supper. You haven't eaten, have you?"

He shook his head. He hadn't had anything but jerky since he started tracking her and the two men.

"You might as well bring your horse into camp, too," she said, sounding like a very sensible young woman, now. "We can't leave until first light, anyway."

He hesitated, wondering if she'd take off when he went to fetch his horse.

"What did you say your name was?" she asked.

"Lancaster."

"Well, Mr. Lancaster," she asked, "where do you think I'm going to go in the dark? You've ruined any chance I had of getting away. I'm not going anywhere but back there with you. It's my only choice right now, do you see?"

He saw. He dragged both bodies off into the dark, and then went to get his horse. She had a plate of bacon and beans waiting for him when he got back.

Chapter Eighteen

He woke to the smell of fresh coffee and eggs. Kate was very cordial in the morning light, her anger totally dissipated.

"I suppose you'll want to bury those two before we get started?" she asked.

"It's the decent thing to do."

"Well, don't expect me to help you," she said. "That's man's work."

"No argument there."

"I'll break camp while you do that, though."

"Fine."

He dug two shallow graves and covered the bodies with stones, without bothering with any kind of marker. When he got back to camp the fire was out, and the coffee pot and plates were stowed away.

"You could have saddled two of the horses," he said.

"I could have," she said. "I decided not to."

Lancaster wondered how Dobbs and Will had traveled with her without strangling her. . . .

They rode mostly in silence, especially after Lancaster decided to force Kate to work. He made her ride drag for a while, told her how to keep the horses moving. Anytime she balked he threatened to leave her out there alone, which got her going again. She may have wanted to get away from Trudy and the others, but going back to them was better than being left alone, apparently.

"You bastard," she swore at him that night after they'd set up camp. They were seated at the fire and she was touching her face. "My skin feels like paper, after getting all that sand and dust in my face all day. And my muscles ache!"

"I know," Lancaster said. "That's why I cooked."

He reached across the fire and handed her a plate.

"Why did you come after me, anyway?" she asked. "What do you care?"

"Actually," Lancaster said, "I was more concerned about the horses. Trudy and the others really need them in order to keep going on to California."

"Who are you kidding?" she asked. "We're not going to get to California. We're all going to die before we get there."

"Who told you that?"

He waited while she grudgingly shoveled some bacon and beans into her mouth and chewed.

"Ted," she said. "Ted Dobbs."

"Is that why you went with him?" he asked. "He convinced you that you'd die, otherwise?"

"No," she said. "I just wanted to get away."

"Well, you picked a poor way to do it," he said. "If they hadn't already raped you, they surely would have soon."

"No," she said, shaking her head. "Ted said he wouldn't let Frank rape me. He said he'd protect me from him."

Lancaster leaned forward and asked, "And who would have protected you from Dobbs?"

That seemed to give her something to think about, and they finished their dinner in silence.

In the morning Lancaster decided there would be no breakfast.

"I'm hungry," Kate complained.

"Here."

"Beef jerky for breakfast?"

"I want to get back to Council Bluffs tonight," he

said. "That means leaving now and not stopping until we get there."

She pulled on her boots, which she had removed in order to sleep more comfortably.

"Ted and Frank didn't drive me this hard."

"Ted and Frank didn't know anyone was trailing them," he told her. "That's the only reason I caught up so quickly."

"Did you really have to kill them?" she asked.

"Or let them kill me."

"How did you do that?"

"Do what?"

"Kill two men? I thought if you were outnumbered—"

He decided to try and scare her and see what happened.

"It's what I do, Kate," he said. "I was prepared to kill them. They were not prepared for me."

"So . . . you intended to kill them?"

"I intended to kill them if I had to, and I did. They didn't give me a choice."

She stared at him for a few moments, and he thought his words might have had the desired effect.

"Let's get mounted up," he said. "We've got a long way to go today, and I want to be there by nightfall."

She put on her hat and mounted Bristow's horse without any help from Lancaster. He mounted his own and got the other dozen horses moving. He'd thrown Dobbs' and Will's saddle horses in with the others. He figured Trudy and her group might as well make a profit.

"You ready?" he asked Kate.

She nodded, but didn't look at him. He thought she'd be a lot easier to take, today.

Chapter Nineteen

Trudy knew she should have told Lancaster that Kate had gone with Will and Dobbs willingly. The children didn't know, but Martha and Donna knew. Now Trudy wasn't sure how Kate would react to being brought back—and she had no doubt that Lancaster would bring her back. He was that kind of man—the kind who would accomplish what he set out to do. He'd bring back the horses, and Kate, and then they would be back on the trail, heading for California.

For the entire trip to this point, Trudy had been frightened. The whole thing was her idea. She was the one who heard about the miners, she was the one who had written to them, and to whom they had written back, telling her how excited they were about becoming instant family men. It was she who had convinced Martha and Donna to make the trip with her, and it was the three of them who had chosen the children who would come with them.

At first she had been elated, but then the fear had set in. The elation faded, and the fear stayed—and then the guilt over the children who had already died along the way. Two of them were not even five years old when they succumbed to a fever, and eleven-year-old Todd had been bitten by a snake and died instantly. And eight-year-old Ally, who had fallen out of the wagon and broken her leg, could just as easily have been killed.

And now Mr. Bristow was dead.

The only thing that had kept Trudy from succumbing completely to the fear had been having Bristow along. While he was there he was in charge, but now he was gone and, suddenly, it was she who was in charge. Donna was looking to her for guidance, and even Martha—older by ten years—was looking to her. And even the children seemed to sense that it was Trudy who was the leader now.

But Trudy had now gone beyond frightened. She was petrified with fear, and could not let anyone know about it. But she knew that the only way she was going to be able to keep the fear in check, keep it from totally overpowering her, was to get Lancaster to take them to California.

She knew as soon as she met him that he was the

man she'd been looking for, hoping for, ever since they had left Philadelphia. He was the westerner she'd been hoping would come along to make them safe. And he was even more than she had hoped for. After Aaron told her what had happened in town she had immediately dissolved into a quivering mass inside—but then she met Lancaster, and she knew he was their salvation—her salvation. She was terribly sorry that Bristow was dead, and she felt guilty that she was only too happy to trade Bristow for Lancaster, but she now knew she had to find some way—any way—to get Lancaster to go with them when they left Council Bluffs.

She was going to have to say anything . . . do anything . . . to make that happen.

"Miss Bennett?"

It was Aaron, standing across the campfire from her, staring at her with those big eyes.

"Yes, Aaron?"

He pointed and said, "Somebody's coming."

Chapter Twenty

Lancaster could see the campfires in the distance. It was almost totally dark, and if not for the fires he would have called their progress to a halt for the night. They had just made it.

He turned and rode back to the rear of the tattered remuda.

"Kate," he said, "we're here." He pointed to the fire so she could see it.

"Thank God!" she said. "I'm so exhausted."

This was good, he thought. She'd be grateful to get down from her horse—grateful, and happy to be back.

"Come on," he said, "let's push them one last time."

* * *

Lancaster stopped the horses short of trampling their way into camp and made Kate help him secure them before allowing her to walk into camp. The minute she saw Trudy she rushed into her arms and dissolved into tears.

"He killed them!" she cried. "He killed them both!"

Trudy looked at Lancaster over the girl's head.

"They didn't give me a choice," he said.

Trudy nodded and mouthed "thank you," to him.

Then Aaron shouted, "Kate's back!" and all the children came running to embrace her, some of the little girls crying along with her. Kate went to her knees to hug them each individually while Donna and Martha looked on, the campfire glitteringly reflected in the tears in their eyes.

Trudy walked over to Lancaster and said, "I'm sorry."

"You should be," he said. All the way back he'd been thinking about what to say to her. "Not knowing that she willingly went with them could have gotten me killed."

She covered her mouth with her hands and said, "I'm sorry, I—I didn't think."

"Trudy," he said, "if you're going to survive out here that's the one thing you're going to have to learn how to do—think."

"I know, I know," she said. "I'm just—I can't—I'm so grateful—"

"Never mind," he said. "Kate's exhausted and we could both use some hot food."

"Of course, of course."

"And, if you don't mind," he said, "I'll camp here tonight with you and the others."

"Of course we don't mind." She waited a moment, then asked, "And tomorrow?"

He hesitated, then said, "Tomorrow is tomorrow. We'll think about it then."

The small flower of hope she'd been harboring inside of her suddenly burst into full bloom.

Chapter Twenty-one

Lancaster woke to the sound of children laughing. He removed his hat from his eyes and squinted at the morning sun. He looked up and found three children, a boy and two girls, all about four or five years old, staring down at him.

"Good morning," he said.

The two girls turned and ran away instantly. The boy stared at him for a few more moments, scratched his nose, then turned and calmly walked away.

Lancaster sat up and looked around. At one of the fires he saw Kate making breakfast with Donna, and both were laughing happily. He wondered if Kate was acting, or if she was really glad to be back.

Perhaps she was even surprised to find how happy she was to be back.

Or maybe she simply figured she had no choice. Maybe she would simply bide her time and seize the very next opportunity that came along to run again.

Well, it didn't matter to him, because he wouldn't be along to see. He was going to have breakfast with the group today, and then he was going to be on his way.

Trudy watched as Lancaster got to his feet and trudged over to the campfire. Kate smiled at him and handed him a steaming cup of coffee. The younger woman had confided to Trudy last night that she was afraid of him after watching how easily Lancaster had killed Will and Dobbs, and had no feeling about it afterward. Trudy thought that if Lancaster was going to be with them as they moved on to California, it might not be a bad idea to have Kate be so fearful of him.

Lancaster came walking over to her, bringing his hot cup of coffee with him.

"Good morning," she greeted.

" 'Morning." He turned to look one more time at Kate, then back at Trudy. "She seems very happy, this morning."

97

"You know you scared her to death, yesterday."

"That's good," he said. "I was trying to. I think it will make her easier to handle."

"For a while, anyway," Trudy agreed.

"I'll help you hitch up the teams this morning," he said.

"We won't be leaving this morning."

"Oh? Why not?"

"We can't drive all the wagons," she told him. "We're three men short."

"Bristow was going to try to hire some men from town?"

"I believe he was going to see if he could find someone," she said. "He wasn't very confident in Mr. Dobbs and Mr. Will."

"Well, he turned out to be right about that," Lancaster said. "I guess I could ride into town and make some inquiries . . . but how much can you pay?"

"Not much," she said. "I think Mr. Bristow was hoping he could find a man who might be heading that way and would like the company, and would work for meals."

"That won't be easy," Lancaster said, "but I'll take a ride into town and see what I can scare up. I can stop in and see the sheriff, too. I need to tell him what happened with Dobbs and Will."

"We appreciate anything you can do," Trudy said, "not that you haven't already done enough for us."

"Asking some questions in town is not going to be a hardship, Trudy," he said. "In fact, maybe you'd like to ride in with me? I'll buy you lunch."

She hesitated a moment and he said, "But of course, if you're busy—"

"No," she said, "no, not at all. That's a very nice invitation, Lancaster. I'd like to take you up on it."

"Good," he said. "I'll saddle a horse for you."

Lancaster and Trudy rode into Council Bluffs together. From the look of the streets everything was back to normal. At least, no one was hanging from any of the street lamps.

"That café looks like a good place for lunch," Lancaster said, pointing to a place on the main street.

"All right."

"Let's go and see the sheriff first, though."

They came to a stop in front of the sheriff's office and Lancaster dismounted quickly to help Trudy down from her horse. She beat him to it, though, and was already on the ground. She had dressed for riding with boots and man's jeans, and she looked quite fetching astride a horse. He didn't tell her, though. It was already plain to him that she did not know how to handle compliments.

He opened the door to the office and allowed her to precede him. Sheriff Lockwood looked up from his desk as they entered and smiled when he recognized them. He took whatever he was writing and turned it over.

"Good afternoon to both of you," he said, standing. He almost bowed, and Lancaster figured if he had been wearing his hat he would have doffed it. Trudy inspired that kind of behavior in a man. How could she not know that?

"Afternoon, Sheriff," Lancaster said.

"Miss Trudy," Lockwood said.

"Sheriff."

"You get all them supplies squared away?"

"Yes, thank you." Trudy noticed Lancaster's questioning look. "While you were away the sheriff was kind enough to bring out the supplies that Mr. Bristow had bought before he was, uh, killed."

"I see."

"Did you catch up to those varmints?" Lockwood asked.

"Yes, I did," Lancaster said. "I got back the horses and the girl. Unfortunately, I had to kill both of them."

"Got them outside on their horses?" the lawman asked. "Might be a reward."

"No," Lancaster said. "I buried them." Luckily, he didn't have a bounty hunter's mentality. It never occurred to him to tie the bodies to their horses and bring them back with him. He had enough trouble driving ten horses and a reluctant girl.

"Well, no matter," Lockwood said. "They deserved what they got, I'm sure."

"So there won't be any need for an inquest of any kind?" Lancaster asked.

"Not that I can see," Lockwood said. "Uh, by the way, there was a reward for Sam Quitman and his men. You gunned 'em, so you're entitled to it. Come to five hundred dollars."

"Oh, my," Trudy said. "Five hundred dollars for killing a man?"

"Three men," Lockwood corrected, "but yes, Ma'am, that's what it amounts to."

"Well . . ." Lancaster's first instinct was to turn it down, but then he thought better of it. "I tell you what, Sheriff. I'll take the money, but I'm going to turn it over to Trudy, here, to finance the rest of her trip."

"Oh, no!" she said, appalled. "I couldn't take that money—"

"You ladies need this money to get those kids to California," Lancaster said, "and I consider that Bristow died for it."

"Still—"

"I think you should take it," Lancaster said, "for the kids."

"I agree," Lockwood said.

She stared at them for several moments, then said, "It doesn't seem decent . . . but I will take it, for the children." She looked at Lancaster. "Once again you're doing more than you should."

"I'm happy to do it," he said. "Sheriff, Trudy and I are having lunch in town. Would you like to join us?"

"Uh, I'd like to, but I have some things to attend to. Stop in again before you leave, though." He took a slip of paper from the top desk of his drawer. "If you'll sign this, Lancaster, I'll have the money waiting for you when you come by."

Lancaster signed the chit.

"When will you be leaving, Miss Trudy?" Lockwood asked.

"Well . . . we were going to look for some men to drive our wagons, and with this money we'll now be able to pay them decently. We'd like to leave in the morning, if we find the men we need."

Lockwood scratched his head.

"Don't know that there's anyone in town who'd take the job."

"No strangers passing through?" Lancaster asked.

"Not since you arrived. Ask around, though. You might find somebody."

"Well," Lancaster said to Trudy, "let's have lunch first and then we can see about hiring some men." He took her arm. "The café across the street okay for food, Sheriff?"

"It's as good as any place in town."

"Okay, then we'll see you later."

"I'll have the money waiting."

"Thank you so much for your kindness, Sheriff."

"It's my pleasure, Ma'am."

"Sheriff," Lancaster said, shaking the man's hand.

As they stepped outside and started across the street to the café she asked, "Why would he want to stay on as sheriff in a town where they were going to allow him to be hanged?"

"I wonder that same thing myself, Trudy."

Chapter Twenty-two

"We've talked about me all during lunch," Trudy Bennett said to Lancaster. "You know I was a teacher in Philadelphia before I started working for the orphanage."

"And that you worked both jobs because you love kids."

She looked at him over her coffee cup. They each had the remnants of a piece of pie in front of them.

"But I know nothing about you," she said. "You're a mystery man, and I think you like it that way."

"Actually," Lancaster said, "I don't."

"Then tell me," she said. "You alluded to some things you're not proud of doing. Were you . . . an outlaw?"

"Let's just say I wasn't always on the right side

of the law," Lancaster said, "but I was never quite an outlaw."

"Gunfighter, then?"

"That's an eastern term," he said, "but accurate, I guess."

"So that's why you were able to kill the three men who were trying to hang the sheriff," she said, "and both Mr. Will and Mr. Dobbs. Because of your prowess with a gun?"

"Prowess," he repeated. "Never heard it put that way before."

"Remember," she said, "I was a teacher." She smiled.

"Trudy," he said, "if I was to tell you everything about myself, about my past, you might not want to be my friend, anymore."

"I can't imagine that," she said, frowning. "You've been wonderful to us. You saved the sheriff's life when you needn't have gotten involved. Only one kind of man does that."

"What kind?"

"The good kind."

He hesitated, then said, "You'll excuse me if I'd like you to go on thinking that a little longer."

She stared at him for a few moments, then said, "All right. I'll stop prying . . . for now."

"Why don't we see if the sheriff has collected your money yet?" he asked. "Then we can try to get you some drivers."

*   *   *

"Here is your money," Lockwood said. He handed an envelope to Lancaster, who in turn gave it to Trudy. She looked inside and caught her breath.

"I don't know what to say."

"There's no need to say anything," Lockwood replied. He looked at Lancaster. "I asked around about drivers and got no takers. You can go ahead and try. I have a proposition for you, though."

"What's that?"

Lockwood hesitated, casting a look at Trudy, who was still looking at the cash inside the envelope.

"Maybe we can step outside and talk about it," he said.

Trudy looked up at them, then, a questioning look on her face.

"Go ahead, then," she said. "Have your secrets. I'll just have a seat and wait here."

"We'll be right back," Lockwood assured her, and then ushered Lancaster to the door.

Trudy sat behind the sheriff's desk and, for lack of anything better to do, began to snoop. The desk was covered with papers, some of which were wanted posters. She started to go through them, appalled at some of the crimes the men had committed, and the amounts of money that were offered for their capture—dead or alive. It wasn't until she came to one particular poster, though, that she gasped and commenced to read every word. . . .

"What's on your mind, Sheriff?"

"First of all, call me Ben," the lawman said.

Lancaster agreed, even though he didn't expect to see the man again once he left Council Bluffs.

"All right, Ben," Lancaster said, "Spill it. What's this proposition you mentioned?"

"I'd like to come with you when you leave Council Bluffs," Lockwood said.

"I usually ride alone."

"No," the other man said, "I mean with you and Miss Bennett and the rest. I can drive a wagon."

Lancaster frowned. "What the hell are you talking about? I'm not going with them."

"You're not?"

"Whatever gave you that idea?"

"Well . . . the way you look at Miss Bennett, and everything you've done for them . . . I just assumed. . . ."

"Well, you assumed wrong."

"You're going to let them go alone?"

"I was going to try to find them some drivers," Lancaster said, "but since you want to go with them—"

"I thought we'd both go," Lockwood said. "Between the two of us we can get them where they're going safely."

Lancaster shook his head.

"I've spent enough time here," he said. "I have to get on—"

"Where?" Lockwood asked. "Where have you to go?"

The question was a salient one. Lancaster was only a year off the bottle, a year away from his dreams of his ghost with blue eyes. For that year he'd been drifting from town to town, no definite destination in mind. He wasn't even sure what he was going to do with his life.

"These people need help, Lancaster," Lockwood said.

"I've already helped them."

"And me, I know," Sheriff Lockwood said, "but they need more help, still."

"And you're willing to give up your badge?"

"Like you said," Lockwood replied, "they were going to watch while I was hanged. What do I owe them? Maybe I can get a job as a lawman in California."

Lancaster frowned and looked across the street. Actually, he was just looking off into the distance, not seeing anything particular. Trudy, her companions and the children surely did need help. He thought about the way the children looked at him— especially the boy, Aaron, who had been so fearful that he would die, like Bristow did.

And then there was Trudy Bennett, beautiful, warm, responsible, caring. . . .

"All right, Ben," Lancaster said. "Let's seen if we can get all these people to California."

Trudy read the wanted poster several times. Even though it was obviously out of date, it told her things she probably should have heard from Lancaster, himself.

As the two men opened the door to come back into the office Trudy hurriedly folded the poster and tucked it away in the envelope with the money. She stood up, moved away from the desk and put her hands behind her back.

Lancaster and Ben Lockwood reentered the office and found Trudy patiently waiting for them.

"Well," she asked, "have you gentlemen come to some sort of a decision?"

Lockwood looked at Lancaster, leaving it to him to tell her their news.

"Trudy, Lockwood has decided to give up his badge and move on," he said. "So there's no need for you to look for drivers. We've decided to drive you and the children to California—if you'll have us."

"If we'll have you?" Trudy repeated. "We wouldn't have it any other way."

Chapter Twenty-three

As it turned out they did leave Council Bluffs for California the next day, but there was still some things to be settled before they turned in the night before.

First, since Trudy had five hundred dollars she offered to pay Lancaster and Ben a hundred each. Both men refused the money and suggested she stock up on more supplies, instead. So they all shopped at the general store, and loaded the supplies onto a rented buckboard, which Ben said he'd return. He intended to resign as sheriff by handing his badge right to Mayor Fred Hansen, who had been one of the people who was going to watch him hang.

They drove the supplies out to the camp and unloaded them with the help of all the women and the children, and then Ben drove it back to town, promising to return before dark with his horse and his belongings.

"This isn't right, Ben," Mayor Hansen said. "You can't jut run out on a town that elected you sheriff."

"This town ran out on me long before this, Fred," Ben said. "You were one of the people who were happy to see me hang."

"Happy . . ." Hansen said. "That's putting it strongly, Ben. We . . . there was nothing we could do—"

"Against three men?"

"It was your job to handle those men."

Ben took off his tin star and dropped it on the desk, "Well, it's not my job anymore, Mr. Mayor."

He turned and headed for the door.

"Ben, Quitman's brothers are on their way here!"

The statement stopped him before he could get through the door. He turned and looked at Fred Hansen.

"Brothers?"

Hansen nodded.

"There were six, and Sam was the baby," Hansen said. "The others are on the way here. We just got word today."

"And when were you gonna tell me *that*?" Ben demanded.

"Well . . ."

"You weren't, were you?" Ben asked. "You were gonna let them ride in here and kill me."

"Well . . ."

"You stink, Mr. Mayor," Ben said. "It's a stink that's gonna take me a while to get out of my nostrils."

Ben opened the door, and Hansen stood up.

"I'll tell them about you, Ben," Hansen said. "About you and Lancaster. I won't let them destroy this town."

"You know something, Mr. Mayor?" Ben said. "No matter what you tell them, I don't think you'll be able to stop them. So you better find yourself a real good man to pin that badge on."

Ben was still fuming when he rode into camp. Very quickly he told Lancaster about Sam Quitman's brothers, but he did it in private. No need to worry the women about it.

"That changes things," Lancaster said.

"How?"

"We can't endanger these women and children," Lancaster said. "We can't go with them as long as the Quitman brothers are after us. And we ought to go our separate ways, to split them up."

"I don't agree," Ben said. "We can handle them better together. Besides which, Fred Hansen doesn't know that we're leaving with these people. They'll be looking for our trails on horseback, not driving five wagonloads of women and children to California."

Lancaster thought a moment, then said, "We have to tell them."

"Tell who?"

"Trudy and the others. They have a right to know what they might be letting themselves in for by having us come along with them."

"Fine," Ben said. "Tell them. Let them make the decision. They know they're better off with us than without us."

Lancaster and Ben Lockwood collected Trudy, Martha and Donna around the campfire, and Kate came over to stand next to Trudy. She stared at Lancaster as if his every mood were important to her, only Lancaster wasn't so sure she was afraid of him, anymore.

"Sheriff—I mean, Ben has something he wants to tell you all," Lancaster said.

Ben related to the women his conversation with the mayor when he turned in his badge. He gave them every word, right down to the remaining five Quitman brothers.

The four women then looked at Lancaster, waiting for the next step.

"Do you see?" he asked. "By staying with you, we might be putting you in danger."

"We knew when we started this trip that there

113

would be danger," Trudy said. "We discussed it, and decided that the trip was worth it. Why should this be any different?"

She looked at the other women.

"Martha?"

"We're better off with Lancaster and Ben than without them."

"Donna?"

"I agree," she said. "And I also agree with Ben. These men will be looking for one or two men on horseback. Why in the world would they come after us?"

Trudy looked at the youngest of the women and asked, "How do you feel about this, Kate?"

"Lancaster will kill them," she said. "If they come after us and catch up to us, he'll kill them, no matter how many there are."

Kate's faith in his ability to kill five men was underwhelming, to say the least, but Lancaster let that go, for the moment.

"All right, then," he said. "We'll be heading out at first light. Trudy, after you get the children to bed Ben and I would like to discuss with all of you the route we'll take, and the rotation of who will drive what wagon, and when."

"All right," she said. "We should be ready within the hour."

"Good."

The women dispersed to take care of the children.

Trudy held back after sending Kate off to see to the smallest one.

"I think," she said to Lancaster, "that Kate's fear of you might have turned into something else."

Lancaster wasn't at all sure that was a good thing.

Chapter Twenty-four

Trudy came to sit with Lancaster and Ben Lockwood to discuss their route over coffee. Luckily, before his death Bristow and the other men had
already gotten the wagons across the river, so they
didn't have to deal with that.

"What about the other ladies?" Lancaster asked.

"They've said they'll go along with whatever we
decide," Trudy assured him. "They just want to get
there, they don't particularly care how."

"All right, then," Lancaster said. He looked at
Ben, who simply shrugged, indicating that Lancaster should go ahead and take the lead. Ben had
given up his badge, and the authority, as well.

Lancaster handed Trudy a cup of coffee. "Maybe

116

you better tell us exactly where we're going, and why?"

"Well, I told you that I had corresponded with a man from California," she said. "He and his partners are in Shasta County."

"North of Sacramento," Lancaster said.

"Yes," she said. "According to Mr. Kerry, the man I corresponded with, it's somewhere between Redding and Whiskytown."

"Somewhere near the Trinity Mountains?" Lancaster asked.

"Yes," she said. "You know the area?"

"A little."

"Much more than I do."

"Or me," Ben said.

"Now, Kerry and his people . . . they're miners?"

"Yes," she said.

"Gold?" Ben asked.

"California was pretty much out of the gold rush by the mid-sixties," Lancaster said. "If they've told you they're gold miners they haven't exactly been honest."

"No," she said, "they haven't been lying. According to Mr. Kerry they're doing something called hard rock mining in some played out gold mines."

"I don't know what that is," Ben said.

"I do," Lancaster said. "Some of the gold mines

also yielded other kinds of rock. In fact, in New Mexico when they found gold they also found diamonds."

"Mr. Kerry said they had found several veins of other kinds of ore," she told them. "He said they had to work hard to get it out, and that did not leave much time to build families."

"Okay," Lancaster said, "it sounds like you know what you're doing as far as where you're going and why."

"I—we—did not come to this decision lightly, Lancaster," Trudy said. "I exchanged letters with Mr. Kerry for over a year before we decided to make the trip."

"All right," Lancaster said. "Can you tell me what route Bristow was taking you on?"

"Not really," she said. "I'm afraid we pretty much put ourselves in his hands. I know we came through Ohio and Indiana, then Illinois and Missouri."

"Pretty straightforward," Lancaster said. "If we simply continue west from here we'll go all the way through Nebraska, then Wyoming and a bit of Utah before we reach Nevada. After that it's northern California."

"It sounds good to me," Ben said. "I'm just along for the ride, after all."

Lancaster looked at Trudy. "I know you've been

on the trail for months, but we're still talking about months to go."

"We know that," she said, "but I have to tell you we're going to feel a lot safer with you and Sheriff Lockwood along."

"Not a sheriff, anymore," Ben reminded her.

"It doesn't matter," she said. "You're an ex-lawman and that's more than we knew about the other men."

"What about Bristow?" Lancaster asked.

"Mr. Bristow was honest and trustworthy, but he did not have good taste when it came to hiring other men. Mr. Will and Mr. Dobbs are testament to that fact."

"So, you trust me and Lancaster?" Ben asked.

"Yes."

"Why?'

"As I said," she replied, "you are an ex-lawman, and you put yourself in danger for the townspeople. An untrustworthy man would not have done that."

"And Lancaster?"

"Mr. Lancaster has already proved himself," she said. "He's helped you, and he's already helped us."

"Okay," Lancaster said, "We've established that we can all be trusted. Now let's figure out who drives what tomorrow."

"What about the horses?" Ben asked.

"What about them?" Lancaster asked.

"They've been through a lot," he said. "Are they gonna get us where we want to go?"

"I've examined them," Lancaster said, "and the answer's no, but they'll be okay for a while. I think at some point we might buy some new ones, and we might also consolidate down to four wagons, or three."

"That would be pretty crowded," Trudy said.

"It's just a thought, Trudy," Lancaster said. "Let's just see what happens as we go along. For now, let's figure out how we'll place the wagons, and who'll drive what. . . ."

At first light they had a quick breakfast because Trudy said the children had to eat. This was Lancaster's first indication that things would not always go the way he wanted them to. If he had been traveling with a bunch of men they would have broken camp and moved out without breakfast. Traveling with a group of women and children was going to be very different.

Lancaster determined that, if need be, all four women—including eighteen-year-old Kate—could drive a wagon. However, he decided to start with himself driving the lead wagon, and Ben Lockwood driving the last one. The three wagons in between would be driven by Trudy, Martha and Donna.

The children were spread evenly throughout the five wagons, with Aaron riding shotgun alongside

Lancaster, and Kate riding next to Ben. There would be times when Lancaster would prefer to be on horseback—and the same for Ben Lockwood—but at least in the beginning, he was going to drive the lead wagon.

"Wagons ho!" he shouted, waving his arm so the other drivers would see it. After that he flicked his reins at the horses, putting them all under way.

Chapter Twenty-five

Day Five

Five days later the Quitman brothers rode into Council Bluffs.

In the lead was Big Jed Quitman. Whether they were brothers or a gang Jed was the leader. In his mid-forties, he'd been father and mother to the other boys ever since their Ma and Pa died. Actually, unlike the other boys, Jed had lost two mothers. His mother had been his father's first wife, but she had died of a fever when he was four. It took his Pa five years to get over her death, meet someone and marry again. He had five more children with Jed's stepmother—all of them boys—before she was killed when kicked in the head by a horse. Losing two wives was too much for the old man, and he drank himself to death after that, although it took him six years to do it. At twenty-two Jed was left to raise his five half-brothers—Emmett, fourteen; Frank, twelve; Peter, ten; Johnny, eight; and Sam, six.

Ten years later the Quitman brothers started robbing banks and trains, taking what they wanted when they wanted it. For twelve years the Quitmans had marched across the west, with no law able to stop them. Sheriffs, marshals, even Pinkertons had tried. They were harder to find and kill than the James boys were.

Now one of them was dead. Sam, the baby, the headstrong one. If he hadn't gone off on his own with a couple of friends of his, determined to make his own way, he'd be alive right now and riding with his brothers.

And they wouldn't even have to be in Council Bluffs.

Jed's mother, Lorraine, had been a big, raw-boned woman, which made it all the more ironic that she had succumbed to a fever while the other boys' mother—petite and gentle Mary—had been killed violently. So while the other boys all resembled one another—all under six feet and two hundred pounds—Jed was a bull of a man, like his father had been. More often than not Jed used his large hands to mete out punishment to the boys as they grew up, and even now the others were wary of his anger. They had seen Jed break a man in half more than once during a fight.

Jed Quitman led three of his brothers to the nearest watering hole as they entered town, bringing them to a stop in front of the Black Horse Saloon.

"Johnny," he said, dismounting, "see to the horses."

"What do I do with them?" Johnny asked.

"Take them to the livery stable," Jed said, patiently, "see that they're tended to properly. Come back here with our saddlebags."

The other boys dismounted and handed their reins to Johnny.

"Ain't we gonna talk to the law, Jed?" Frank asked.

"Soon enough," Jed said. "Let's have a drink and something to eat first. Besides, word'll get around soon enough, and the law might come lookin' for us."

Jed mounted the boardwalk, followed by Frank and Pete. Before entering he took off his hat and beat some of the trail dust from his clothes, then glared at his brothers until they did the same. Only then did he lead the way into the saloon.

As soon as the batwing doors opened to admit the three men Ted Ryan, standing behind the bar, knew who they were.

"Ford," he said to the man drinking in front of him.

"Huh?"

"Go and tell Mayor Hansen they're here."

"Who's here?" Ford asked. He was more interested in his whiskey than anything else. All he did was drink whiskey or sweep out the saloon. Doing one kept him in the other.

"The Quitmans!" Ryan hissed. "They're here. Go and tell the mayor."

"I gotta finish my—"

Ryan snatched the whiskey glass from Ford Fargo's hand. "You'll get your drink back after you deliver the message."

"Aw, Ted—"

"Go!"

The man started to turn toward the front door but Ryan grabbed his arm and said, "Go out the back—and hurry!"

"Awright, awright," Ford said, and slipped away to the back door.

Ryan nervously touched the shotgun he kept beneath the bar, but he knew he wasn't going to try and use it. Not against the Quitman brothers. Hell, even if it was just Jed Quitman he'd have been too scared to use it.

He stood tensely behind the bar and waited.

* * *

Jed Quitman stopped just inside the doors to survey the room. He'd kept him and his brothers alive this long by being a careful man. That was something Sam had never appreciated.

It was midday, so the saloon was mostly empty. Jed moved slowly to the bar, with Frank and Pete trailing him. The boys were anxious to find out who had killed their brother, and where they were, but Jed didn't seem to be in much of a hurry. Privately they wondered if this was because Jed was only half brother to Sam. For as long as they had been together the five of them who had the same mother had felt a separation from Jed. Maybe because he was a half brother, or maybe because they thought of him as more father than brother. Whatever the reason they had always had an "us" and "him" relationship with Jed.

But they also knew he was the smart one, the leader, and they had to follow him if anything was going to get done.

If only Sam had kept believing that.

Chapter Twenty-six

Mayor Hansen knew Ford Fargo was the town drunk, but he also knew that Ted Ryan was going to send him a messenger when the Quitman brothers arrived in town.

This was the day.

Hansen left his office and rushed over to the sheriff's office, with Ford Fargo in tow.

"I can't do this, Mayor," Ford kept saying as Hansen dragged him across the street.

"You have to, Ford," Hansen said. "There's no one else."

"B-but I ain't no lawman!"

"You only have to be one for a few hours," Fred Hansen assured him.

"B-but I ain't got no gun—"

"Ford, I'll give you everything you need."

"I need a drink."

Hansen dragged Ford into the sheriff's office and slammed the door shut behind them.

"When this is over I'll get you a whole bottle."

"A whole bottle?" the man asked, his bloodshot eyes widening.

"All for yourself."

"What do I gotta do?"

"Well, first," Hansen said, bringing his hand out of his pocket, "put on this badge. . . ."

"Beer," Jed said to Ryan. "Three."

"Comin' up."

Ryan could see his hands shaking as he drew the three beers. He tried to keep them still as he set the mugs down in front of the three Quitman brothers.

"Why are you so nervous?" Jed asked him.

So much for keeping his hands still.

"Well . . . you're Jed Quitman."

"And that makes you nervous?"

"Sure."

Jed took a sip of his beer, then put it down.

"That makes you a smart man."

"Not so much," Ryan said.

"Don't be modest."

The batwing doors opened and Johnny Quitman

entered, staggering beneath the weight of all their saddlebags. He stumbled to the bar and dropped the bags on top of it.

"Another beer for my other brother," Jed said.

"Comin' up."

He set the beer down in front of Johnny, who grabbed it and guzzled half of it down.

As Ryan started past Jed Quitman, he reached out and grabbed the front of his shirt.

"Did you send a message to somebody?"

"Why would I—" He stopped short when Jed tightened his hold, cutting off his air.

"Okay, okay," Ryan gasped. Quitman loosened his grip just enough. "I sent a message to the mayor."

"Why not the sheriff?" Quitman asked. "The sheriff who killed my brother, Sam?"

"The sheriff didn't kill your brother."

"No? Then who did?"

"A man named Lancaster."

Quitman stared at Ryan for a few moments, then released him.

"I know that name," he said.

"Who is it, Jed?" Pete asked.

"Man with a rep," Quitman said, "at least, a few years ago. I heard he got outdrew and turned into a drunk."

"So how could he kill Sam, then?" Frank asked. "Sam was fast."

"Not as fast as he thought he was," Jed said. "I guess Lancaster didn't become such a drunk, after all."

"So what do we do now?" Johnny asked, wiping foam from his upper lip with his sleeve.

"I guess we'll have to talk to the sheriff," Jed said, "and the mayor, find out where Lancaster went."

"Want us to go get them?" Pete asked.

"No," Quitman said. "I think if we wait right here they'll be along soon." He looked at Ryan. "More beer."

"C-comin' up."

Ford Fargo stopped across the street from the Black Horse Saloon and dug in his heels.

"I can't do this, Mayor."

"Yes, you can, Ford," Hansen said. "You weren't always a drunk."

"I can't remember when I wasn't."

"Give me two hours of your time," Hansen said, "and you can go back to being one."

Ford licked his lips, then touched them.

"A whole bottle?"

"A whole bottle," Hansen confirmed.

Ford Fargo shifted the gunbelt on his hips. He hadn't worn a gun in a very long time. He hoped nobody expected him to use it.

Chapter Twenty-seven

"We haven't covered much ground in five days," Ben Lockwood said to Lancaster.

"We're doing okay, Ben."

"Not good enough."

The two men regarded each other across the campfire. They had taken to sharing their own fire, letting the women and children crowd around two others. Sometimes they had things to discuss that they didn't want the others to hear.

"And we camped too soon today," Ben said, looking at the sky.

"I know that."

"We're not going to put miles between us and the Quitman brothers this way."

Lancaster scowled. Originally, he had thought

that the horses and wagons they had were, at best, serviceable. Today one of the wheels had snapped and they'd been forced to stop just after midday. Running a wagon train had never been a talent of his. Five days and a mistake was already coming back to bite him on the ass.

"So what do we do?" Ben asked. "Fix it?"

"Either that, or consolidate," Lancaster said. "Move on with four wagons."

"That'll overcrowd them."

"I know," Lancaster said, "and we have nothing to leave behind."

"And even if we did," Ben said, "that would leave a trail a blind man could follow."

"Look behind us, Ben," Lancaster said. "We're already leaving a trail a blind man could follow."

"Well, let's hope the Quitmans don't figure it out," Ben Lockwood said. "If they do come after us it won't take them long to catch up to us."

Kate came over to them with a plate for each of them.

"Thank you, Kate," Ben said.

She nodded, gave Lancaster a shy look, and withdrew. He was confused. This was not the headstrong girl he had retrieved from Will and Dobbs. He wondered if her current behavior was an act, for the benefit of Trudy and the other women. He doubted she'd think she could fool him, not after that two-day ride back.

"Pretty girl," Ben said.

"Don't get attached to her, Ben," Lancaster said. "I think she'll be gone the first chance she gets."

"Why do you say that?"

Lancaster hadn't told Ben about Kate before, so he explained now how she had not been an abductee.

"You mean she went with those men willingly?"

"Yes."

"She's lucky she wasn't raped and left by the side of the road."

"I explained that to her," Lancaster said. "She was still pretty sore that I brought her back."

"I find that hard to believe," Ben said, shaking his head. "She seems so sweet, so innocent. We've been talking quite a bit during the past five days."

"Well," Lancaster said, not wanting to argue the point, "maybe she's different with you."

And maybe her act extended to convincing the ex-lawman, but she and Lancaster knew the truth.

A few moments later Ben had changed places with Trudy, who was seated next to Lancaster, drinking coffee. He was also drinking from the cup she'd brought him.

"Are you worried?" she asked him.

"About what?"

"The men you said would be looking for you," she said. "Do you think they'll catch us?"

"Trudy," he said, "I don't even know if they're after us. Nobody in town knows for sure that we left with you."

"Someone might guess, though," she said. "After all, we bought all those supplies—"

"Yes," he said, "yes, someone might guess."

"And then they'll come after us," she said. "Perhaps you and Ben should go off on your own."

"That won't solve anything," Lancaster said. "If they're following the wagons they might just keep following them. We don't want them to catch up to you and find out we're not with you."

"What would they do to us?" she asked. "We can't harm them. And we didn't do anything to their brother."

"They might be the kind of men who would . . . take advantage of you, and the other women," Lancaster said.

She understood. He could see it in the widening of her eyes.

"But . . . what would they do to the children?" she asked, after a moment.

"I honestly don't know, Trudy," he said. "All I know is that we're going to stick together. Okay?"

She hesitated, then put her hand on his arm and said, "Okay. You're the boss."

Chapter Twenty-eight

Jed Quitman turned as the batwing doors opened again. Two men entered, one wearing a badge. The other man wore a three-piece suit and had the look of a politician. Probably the mayor. The first man looked like he was wilting beneath the weight of the badge.

"Ah," Jed said, "the local law."

He was not looking at Ted Ryan or he would have seen the bartender's look of utter surprise. He'd sent Ford Fargo to take a message to the mayor. He certainly had not expected the town drunk to reappear as the sheriff of Council Bluffs.

The few other men who were in the saloon were registering the same surprise, but a hard look to each from the mayor caused them to hold their tongues.

"Who's the stuffed shirt?" Peter asked Ryan.

"That's the mayor," Ryan said, "Mayor Hansen."

"Mr. Mayor!" Jed called.

Fred Hansen's head swiveled so fast Ten Ryan was surprised it didn't fall off.

"You and the sheriff come over and have a drink on the Quitman brothers," Jed called. "It's the least you can do after letting our brother get killed in your fair town."

Jed watched as the two men approached the bar. The man with the badge had bloodshot eyes and his hands were shaking. He was also constantly licking his lips.

"Sheriff," Jed said, "you look like a man who could use a drink." He turned to Ryan. "Whiskey for the sheriff, bartender."

"The sheriff doesn't drink on du—" the mayor started, but the sheriff cut him off.

"Thank you kindly, Mr. Quitman," he said. "I'd be happy to have a drink with you."

"And you, Mr. Mayor?" Jed Quitman asked.

"Well . . . sure . . ."

"Two whiskeys, bartender."

Ted Ryan set two glasses on the bar and filled them both to the brim with whiskey. The "sheriff" didn't have to be asked twice. He grabbed one of

the glasses and downed it in one convulsive move-
ment, then wiped his mouth with the back of his
sleeve.

"Thank you, Mr. Quitman," he said. "That went
down mighty smooth."

"I'm glad you enjoyed that drink, Sheriff," Jed
Quitman said, "because it was your last."

With that Jed pulled his gun and shot Ford Fargo
right between the eyes.

Chapter Twenty-nine

One of the things Lancaster established early on was that, when they stopped to camp, everybody had a job to do. On the first night he took Aaron and two other boys about the same age and showed them how to picket the horses so that they wouldn't slip away during the night. The next night he let them do it themselves—or at least think they were. The truth was, he was watching them from a distance the whole time.

The women built the fires, but it was the men who went out and collected the wood. It wasn't until after their meal that everyone was allowed to do whatever they wanted. Go for a walk—as long as they went in groups, and with one older boy with them—read, sew, relax, whatever they wanted to do.

Since they'd stopped early on this day, however, the meal they had would not be their last, so extra wood had to be collected. Also, Lancaster and Ben Lockwood had to see what they could do about the busted wheel, so while the others were relaxing—except for the women whose job it was to keep the fires going—the two men were doing anything but.

Lancaster and Ben finally did a patch job on the wheel they thought would hold until they reached the next town—which, by Lancaster's reckoning, would be Columbus.

"It'll probably take us four or five days of steady travel to get there," Lancaster said.

"Think that wheel will hold that long?" Ben asked.

"I hope so. Our only other option is go back to Fremont, and that'll still be about three days."

"We can't go back," Ben said. "We don't know who's on our trail."

"Then the wheel will have to hold until Columbus," Lancaster said. "Then again, we might come to a settlement between here and there where someone could help."

"There are a few between here and there," Ben

said. "I've heard about them from travelers, but I've never been to any."

"When's the last time you traveled this way?" Lancaster asked.

"Can't remember," Ben said. "I didn't leave Iowa that much as sheriff. Heck, hardly the county. Once in a while I took a ride to Omaha to blow off some steam."

Omaha was too far back, even farther than Fremont. It was a big city, but not an option.

"Better get some rest," Lancaster said. His own muscles were aching from wrestling with the weight of the wagon. He figured as a lawman Ben probably wasn't used to that kind of work, either.

"I could use some coffee," Ben said. "I think I'll see if Kate has some going."

Lancaster watched the man walk to one of the fires, where Kate was working. As he watched them talk he wondered if the ex-lawman was going sweet on the girl. She could have been sweet on him, he supposed, but he was still wary of her.

"What are you thinking?"

He turned and saw Trudy standing behind him, her arms folded. She had some of the smaller children around her, and had apparently been out walking with them. They ran ahead of her and in to camp while she stayed with Lancaster.

"I'm thinking about Kate and Ben," he said.

"Do you think they like each other?" she asked.

"I think he likes her, but I think she might be acting like she likes him." He looked at her. "She's crafty, Trudy."

"I know she went with those men willingly, Lancaster," Trudy said, "but Kate's a good girl."

"She's not a girl," he said, "she's a young woman. I think she's starting to understand that she can get things she wants from men, Trudy, by using the fact that she's become a woman."

"You might be right," she said. "She . . . she needs to be taught how to be a woman."

"You can do that for her," he said. "You, or Donna, or Martha, can't you?"

"A mother would do it better," she said, "and none of us are her mother."

"Closest to it, I'll bet."

"I'll have to talk to her," Trudy said, nodding to herself. "She's so anxious to be on her own. She was in the orphanage longer than any of the other children. She's tired of doing what she's told."

"Not doing what she's told on this trip could get her killed," Lancaster said. "Make her understand that."

Trudy thought a moment, then said, "You could do that."

"Me?"

She nodded.

"She respects you."

"You could have fooled me."

141

"Since you got back," she said, "her feelings have changed. She was afraid of you, but now she respects you. She watches you, looks to you."

Now he thought a moment, then said, "If you think I could get through to her."

"I do."

"All right," he said. "At some point I'll talk to her."

"It might do you both some good," Trudy said, and wandered into camp. He didn't know exactly what she meant by that.

Chapter Thirty

Fred Hansen and Ted Ryan stared down at Ford Fargo's body in stunned silence. The other men in the saloon all remained where they were, afraid that if they moved they'd become the next target.

Jed Quitman holstered his gun and picked up his beer mug. He spoke to the mayor without looking at him.

"I don't know what you thought you'd gain by trying to pass off the town drunk as the sheriff, Mayor," he said, "but looks like all you did was get him killed."

"Jesus," Hansen said, finally able to speak.

"Have your drink, Mayor," Jed said. "It'll do you some good. Bring some color back into your face."

Hansen picked up the whiskey with a shaking

hand and brought it to his mouth. He took a sip and started to return the glass to the bar.

"All of it," Jed Quitman said.

"I—I'm really not a drinker—"

Johnny Quitman nudged the mayor from behind and said, "He said all of it!"

The mayor took a deep breath, tossed off the whiskey and promptly choked on it. The Quitman brothers laughed loudly at the man's red face, but there was no real humor in the sound. Ted Ryan was starting to wonder if he was going to get out of this day alive. He touched the shotgun under the bar, then snatched his hand away.

"Now," Jed Quitman said, "with the phony lawman out of the way why don't you tell me where the real one is?"

"Gone," Hansen gasped, then tried again, but it still came out as a croak. "He's gone."

Jed looked at Hansen, then past him at Johnny.

"Bring the mayor closer to me, Johnny."

"You heard him," Johnny said, shoving the mayor until he almost bumped into Jed.

"Mayor," Jed said, "you better tell me what happened when my brother came to your shit bowl of a town."

The mayor cleared his throat and started talking. . . .

*   *   *

By the time the mayor finished his story Ted Ryan was appalled. Everything the man had said put the blame squarely on former Sheriff Lockwood, and on Lancaster.

"So the jury my brother put together found the sheriff guilty?" Jed asked.

"As sin," Hansen said.

"So he was getting ready to hang the sheriff all legal and proper when this Lancaster stepped in?"

"Exactly."

"And Lancaster killed all three of them? My brother and his men?" Jed asked.

"Yes."

"Fair and square?"

"Well . . . the sheriff had something to do with it," Hansen said.

Jed paused to ponder the story, then rubbed his jaw.

"Sammy was fast with a gun, Jed," Johnny said.

"And he hit what he shot at," Pete added.

"H-he never got a shot off," Hansen said. "Lancaster plugged him real quick."

"Now the big question," Jed said. "Where is your real sheriff?"

"He's not our sheriff, anymore," Hansen said. "He left town."

"And went where?"

Hansen looked at Ryan, as if he expected the bartender to add something to the conversation, but

Ryan remained silent. He was still stunned that the mayor was throwing the two men to the dogs.

"Uh, we're not really sure. . . ."

"And what about Lancaster?"

"He left town at the same time."

"Did they go together?" Jed asked.

"They might have."

Jed pinned Hansen with a hard look.

"You're not being as helpful as I'd like, Mayor," Jed said.

"I-I'm doing the best I can, Mr. Quitman."

"Well, you better come up with a direction those two rode off in, and pronto."

"Uh . . . uh. . . . give me a minute."

Jed showed the mayor his beer mug, which had just enough beer in it to swirl.

"You have until I finish my beer," he said, and then tossed it down, slamming the mug down on the bar so hard it shattered, leaving him with the handle.

"They left with these women and children who were camped out of town. . . ."

After the Quitman brothers left the saloon Ted Ryan asked, "What have you done?"

"I saved this town," Mayor Hansen said.

"You saved your own ass," Ryan said, "and you may have killed those women and children. We don't know that Lancaster and Lockwood went with them."

"Well," Hansen said, "we don't know that they didn't. At least it gives them a trail to follow and takes them away from here."

"And you got poor Ford killed!" Ryan pointed out.

Hansen looked down at the dead town drunk, then around at the other two or three men in the place. He leaned over the bar and said, "Ford's no loss, Ted. This town had to be saved!"

"So you'll just throw everyone else to the wolves?" Ryan asked.

"I'm the Mayor," Hansen said. "I'll do what I have to do to—" He stopped short as the batwing doors opened and Jed Quitman stepped back into the saloon.

Everyone turned to look at him.

"One more thing," Jed said, then drew his gun and shot the mayor dead.

"Jesus—" Ryan said.

Jed holstered his gun and looked at Ryan.

"You keep touching the shotgun you got behind the bar," the man said to him. "You gonna go for it?"

Ryan snatched his hands away from the weapon as if it was on fire and said, "No!"

"Smart man," Jed said. "I'm leaving your town

in one piece, bartender, but if we don't find what we're lookin' for, we may be back."

Ryan didn't know what to say to that. Jed looked down at the two bodies on the floor.

"You better clean up in here."

Chapter Thirty-one

Day Eight

By the middle of the eighth day out from Council Bluffs, Lancaster realized he had definitely over-estimated the condition of the horses and wagons. He wasn't even sure, at this point, that they would make it as far as Columbus. That's why he was very happy to see the smoke up ahead.

"How far do you think?" Ben Lockwood asked.

"A couple of miles," Lancaster said.

They were both standing on the ground, at the head of the column of five wagons.

"What do you want to do?"

"Let's get within a half a mile or so," Lancaster

149

said, "and then I'll ride ahead and see what's there."

"Probably just a settlement," Ben said.

"Anything's better than nothing," Lancaster said. "Might be able to at least pick up a wagon to replace the one with the broken wheel. One more good bump and that wheel's going to go again."

"Okay, then," Ben said.

They both turned and saw Trudy and Martha coming toward them. The others had stayed in the wagons.

"What's wrong?" Trudy asked.

"Nothing," Lancaster said. "Looks like there may be some people up ahead. We're going to wait until we get a little closer and then I'll ride in and see what's what."

"Why don't we just all ride in?" she asked.

"Because we don't know what we'd be riding into, Trudy," Lancaster said.

"We have to be careful," Ben chimed in.

"Because of those men who might be looking for you?" she asked.

"Just on general principle, Trudy," Lancaster said. "It pays to be very careful."

"All right," she said.

Ben started back to his wagon with Martha walking alongside of him. Trudy hesitated.

"We're not doing very well, are we?" she asked.

"If we're not it's my fault," Lancaster said. "We

should have tried for some replacement horses and wagons while we were in Council Bluffs. Or else detoured to Omaha. I'm sorry, Trudy. I'm really not experienced as a wagon master."

"Well," she said, "I'm sure you'll make up for it with your other talents."

As she was walking back to her wagon Lancaster thought she couldn't have possibly meant that as suggestively as it had come out.

Of the Quitman brothers, Jed was the tracker. He crouched over the wagon ruts and examined them, then returned to his horse, collected his reins from Frank and mounted up.

"How far ahead?" Frank asked.

"Maybe three, four days, but they're moving slow," Jed said. "We can cut into that some."

"If we push the horses—" Pete started.

"No need for that, Pete," Jed said. "We can catch up to them pretty easily without punishing the horses."

"I still think we shoulda burned that town to the ground," Johnny said.

"Why?" Jed asked.

Johnny shrugged and said, "Just 'cause."

"Burning an entire town to the ground would be a sure way to get a posse after us."

"We've beaten posses before," Pete said.

"I don't want to have to worry about a posse

151

while we're trying to catch up with the men who killed Sam," Jed said.

"What are we gonna do when we catch 'em?" Johnny asked.

"We're gonna kill 'em," Frank said. "Whataya think? Nobody kills our brother and gets away with it, right Jed?"

"Right," the older Quitman said. "I just wish Sammy hadn't been such an idiot."

"Why you callin' him names?" Johnny complained.

"I'm not callin' him names," Jed said. "I'm statin' a fact. He was an idiot. He was an idiot to go off on his own, and he was an idiot to think he could hang a lawman."

"Sounds like fun to me," Johnny said, and Frank and Pete laughed along with him until Jed turned in his saddle and glared at them.

"Killin' lawmen is a bad idea, boys," Jed said. "You get somebody on your trail for good, then."

"What the hell's the difference?" Frank asked. "We got paper out on us all over the country."

"And we're still alive," Jed said. "You want to take over as leader, Frank?"

Frank shook his head.

"Pete?"

"Not me, Jed."

"How about you, Johnny?" Jed asked. "You want to be in charge for a while?"

"N-no, Jed," Johnny said. "I'm happy to be followin' you."

"Then stop questioning every damn thing I say," Jed said. "We follow these tracks and maintain a nice, even pace. We'll catch up to them, eventually."

"What if it's just wagonloads of women and children, Jed?" Johnny asked. "Then what?"

"More questions, John?"

"Hey, I'm just curious," the younger man said. " 'Sides, I ain't had me a woman in a dog's age."

"Me, neither," Pete said. "Sounds kinda nice, finding us a wagonload of women."

"Don't sound that bad, Jed," Frank said.

"If all we find are a couple of wagonloads of women and children," Jed said, "then we got us sent on a wild goose chase. If that's the case then we're goin' back to Council Bluffs and Johnny's gonna get his wish about burnin' that town to the ground."

"And then what?" Pete asked.

"And then we'd have to start all over again," Jed said. "Me, I kinda hope we find Lancaster and that sheriff with the women and children. That happens we get to kill 'em, and then we still got us a bunch of women." He looked at Frank. "That don't sound so bad after all, now that you mention it."

Chapter Thirty-two

The settlement was called Little Omaha.

But it was a little more than a settlement. As Lancaster rode in he knew this was a town in its infancy. He could see all the signs. New buildings, the smell of newly cut lumber in the air, and the eager looks on the faces of the people he passed. That and the fact that the people did not give him suspicious looks as he rode past them, but smiled, instead.

He was happy to find that apparently, one of the first things the people had done was build themselves a livery. He rode directly to it and dismounted. A man came out immediately, wiping his hands off on a rag and smiling.

"Welcome, stranger," he said. "Always glad to have new people in Little Omaha."

"Are you generally the welcoming committee?" Lancaster asked.

"Folks either stop here first, or at the saloon," the man said. He was in his forties, and from the looks of his hands had been a hard worker most of his life.

"You stop at the saloon, yet?"

"Nope," Lancaster said. "Came right here. This town got a lawman?"

"Not yet," the man said. "You ain't plannin' a bank holdup, are you?"

"No."

" 'Cause if you were, we ain't got one."

"No bank holdup," Lancaster said. "Never did it before, and I don't aim to start now."

"What can I do for you, then?" the man asked. "My name's Ames, by the way, Jerry Ames."

He stuck his hand out to shake and Lancaster obliged. The strength in the man's hand was impressive.

"Put your horse up for you?"

"I don't aim to be here that long, Jerry," Lancaster said. "Just like to see if I can do some business."

"What kind?"

"Horses," Lancaster said, "or a wagon . . . or, failing that, a new wheel."

155

"Can't help you with horses," Ames said. "Maybe one horse. Saddle mount?"

"No, I need one that can be part of a team," Lancaster said, then added, "but, actually, one won't help. Do you have any wagons?"

"A buggy, maybe."

Lancaster shook his head.

"A wagon wheel, then."

"That I might be able to help you with," Ames said. "What size?"

Lancaster dug a piece of paper out of his shirt pocket and handed the measurements to the man.

"Would you want me to put it on for you?"

"If you can."

"You'd have to bring it in," Ames said. "I can't go to it."

"No problem."

"Where is it now?"

"Just outside of town."

"I happen to have three wheels on hand," the man said. "Let me check if any of them match this. Where will you be?"

"Well," Lancaster said, "the saloon, I guess."

"Good choice," Ames said. "My brother Lloyd owns it, and is usually the bartender. Tell him you get one beer on the house."

"I'll do that," Lancaster said. "I'm much obliged. Don't suppose you got another brother working at the general store?"

156

"Sorry," Ames said. "Lloyd's the only brother I got."

"Well," Lancaster said, "if you've got to have one he might as well own and operate a saloon."

"My thoughts exactly," Ames said. "I'll be over in about twenty minutes."

"I'll be waiting," Lancaster said. "Like I said, thanks."

Lancaster was still nursing the same beer when Ames came walking into the saloon. Jerry exchanged a glance with his brother, Lloyd, who had a beer waiting by the time Jerry reached the bar.

"Did you meet my friend?" Jerry asked Lloyd.

"Just enough to give him his beer," Lloyd said. "Guess he don't talk much."

Lloyd looked like he was the larger, but younger brother. As far as not talking, Lancaster had nothing to say. He didn't like to give information away if he didn't have to.

"What about that wheel?" Lancaster asked.

"I've got one that'll fit," Jerry Ames said. "Bring in your wagon and I'll put 'er on for you."

"Good," Lancaster said. He put the mug on the bar, leaving the remnants of his warm beer at the bottom. "Shouldn't take me too long to drive it in."

"We got a hotel, if you need a room, or two," Ames said. "We don't get too many visitors, yet."

"Thanks, but I won't need a hotel. I'll just camp outside of town."

"What brings you this way?'

"Just passing through," Lancaster said.

"On your way to . . . ?"

"Anywhere."

Jerry looked at Lloyd and said, "You're right, he don't talk much, does he?"

"Just enough to get my point across," Lancaster said. "I'll be back."

Outside he stopped and looked up and down the street. A new town with no lawman. Jerry and Lloyd Ames were giving Lancaster some bad feelings, and he didn't know why. Everyone else who passed him on the street gave him a nice, friendly smile, but the Ames brothers didn't seem as sincere to him.

He wondered why he was suddenly running into so many sets of brothers.

Chapter Thirty-three

The Quitman boys were short two brother in Council Bluffs, but a telegram before they left town made sure that they'd meet up when Jed and the boys got to Fremont.

The oddity among the Quitmans was that while Emmett was most like Jed, young Sam had been more like Emmett. Jed and Emmett were the smarter, more capable brothers. Emmett and Sam's similarity was that they wanted to be on their own. The difference was Emmett could be on his own and survive and—obviously—Sam had been unable to do that.

"I ain't seen Emmett in a month of Sundays," Johnny called from the back.

"How can we be sure he's here waitin' for us,

Jed?" Frank asked. "We ain't heard from him, like Johnny says, in a—"

"He'll be here," Jed said.

"Where?" Pete asked, looking down both sides of the street.

"The saloon," Johnny said.

"He's right," Jed replied.

"But which one?" Frank asked.

"Johnny?" Jed said.

"You boys sure don't know yore own brother that well," Johnny said. "The one with the prettiest gals."

Fremont was a good sized town, so the brothers split up to check all the saloons. It was Jed who found him, after tying off his horse in front of the Red Garter Saloon. He knew his brothers would find their way there, eventually, and spot his horse, so he didn't feel any obligation to go and find them. He simply went inside in search of his brother.

"Help ya?" the bartender asked.

"Pretty gals here?" Jed asked.

"The prettiest in town."

It was coming up on three o'clock and the saloon was about half full. He didn't see any girls on the floor yet, though.

"When do they come out?"

"Coupla hours."

"I'm lookin' for a fella looks a little somethin' like

160

me, but younger, mebbe a bit smaller if he ain't put on weight." Jed could never figure out why Emmett most resembled him and not his other, slighter full-blooded brothers.

"I know him," the barkeep said. He put down the glass he'd been cleaning with a dirty rag. "Came in last night, took Vicki upstairs and they ain't neither been seen since."

"Which room?"

The man narrowed his eyes.

"You gonna kill 'im?" he asked. "Shoot up the place?"

"He's my brother."

"I known a man killed his own brother, oncet," the man replied.

"No," Jed said, "I ain't gonna kill him."

"Room two, head of the stairs."

Jed headed for the stairway.

"Better knock loud," the man called. "I tried a few times, but they was makin' too much noise."

Jed shook his head and went up the stairs. Leave it to Emmett to find the loudest gal in the place. He sure liked it when a gal was hollering in his ear.

Jed reached the door to room two and pressed his ear to it. Sure enough he could hear a woman hollering, a man grunting, and bed springs protesting.

He stepped back and slammed the heel of his right boot into the door just below the knob. It flew open and slammed against the wall. First thing he saw was his brother's hairy bare butt pumping up and down, but then Emmett jumped off the bed, grabbed his gun from the bedpost and pointed it at the door.

"Jed?"

The girl on the bed sat up, a look of surprise on her face, and big brown nipples on the biggest pair of breasts Jed had seen in a long time. True to his brother's form, though, she had a real pretty face.

"Get dressed and come downstairs, Emmett."

Emmett uncocked his gun and relaxed.

"You like to scared a year's growth out of me."

"Looks like you got it to spare," Jed said. "I'm gonna buy two beers. You wait too long you're gonna have to drink yours warm."

Emmett stood up straight and returned his gun to his holster.

"I'll be down directly," he said.

"Make it sooner," Jed said. "Barkeep says you been at it all night and all day. You're gonna wear that poor gal out."

"You wanna come in and try to wear me out, mister?" the girl asked, sweetly.

"Sorry, sweet thing," Jed said, "but you'd be the death of me. My old heart wouldn't be able to take it."

"That's my big brother, Vicki," Emmett said, "and he's kinda old."

"Don't look too old to me," she said, turning over so Jed could see her naked butt.

Emmett swatted it immediately, drawing a squeal from her, and said, "Close the door, Jed, if'n you didn't kick it off the hinges. I'll be right down."

Jed pulled the door shut, but he had broken the lock so it remained ajar. He could hear the hollering and bed springs start up again before he got to the head of the stairs.

Chapter Thirty-four

When Lancaster returned to his party he dismounted and accepted a cup of coffee from Trudy. Ben Lockwood had had them make camp, and they had two fires going.

"What'd you find?" Ben asked.

"A new wheel and a man to put it on," Lancaster said, "but I got a bad feeling about the place."

"What kind of feeling?"

"Can't put my finger on it," he said. "It's a new town, people real friendly, but I met these two brothers—"

"Brothers?" Ben asked.

"I know," Lancaster said. "Anyway, one owns the livery and will put the wheel on for us, the other owns the saloon."

"Any law in town?"

"Not yet."

"That don't sound right," Ben said.

"I think I'll drive the wagon in, Ben, and you stay here with the ladies and the kids."

"You're gonna need someone to watch your back."

"Maybe not," Lancaster said. "Maybe I'm just a bit antsy."

"I can go with you," Trudy said. "I can use a gun."

Lancaster considered the offer for a few minutes, then rejected it.

"I don't think I want the Ames brothers getting a look at you, Trudy," he said.

"Why not?"

"Because you're too damned beautiful," he said. "You got the kind of looks that do something to a man, and I already have a bad feeling about those two."

Trudy blushed and remained silent. Off to one side Kate said something to Donna, and giggled.

"I'll chance going in alone, Ben," Lancaster said. "I'd take you along, but I really don't want to leave the women and children out here by themselves."

"Okay," Ben said.

They separated the wagon in question from the others and Lancaster tied his horse to the back of it.

"If you're not back by nightfall I'm comin' in lookin' for you," Ben said, as they were away from the others.

"Fair enough," Lancaster said. "We should have enough light for me to be able to get the wheel fixed and get back here before dark, but if I'm not I'll probably welcome you."

Chapter Thirty-five

Frank and Peter had found Jed in the Red Garter and had beers in front of them by the time Emmett made his way down to the saloon. His beer was warm, but he drank it anyway, then slapped the boys on the back.

"Good to see you boys," he said. "Where's Johnny?"

"Still wanderin' around lookin' for you," Pete said. "He'll find his way here."

"A damn shame about Sammy," Emmett said. He raised his mug. "Here's to 'im."

They drank, him finishing off his warm beer.

"I'm gettin' another?"

"We're good," Jed said, before the other boys could speak.

167

As Emmett went to the bar for a cold one Jed said, "I don't want you boys gettin' likkered up, understand?"

"Aw, Jed—" Pete said.

"Understand?"

"Sure, Jed," Frank said, and Pete nodded. "We understand—but how come Emmett can drink?"

"Emmett can handle it," Jed said, "you two can't—and Johnny's even worse."

Before the boys could reply Emmett returned with his cold beer.

"So, tell me what happened when you went to Council Bluffs?" he said.

Jed gave Emmett the story from start to finish, ending with the shooting of the mayor.

"You should have burned the town to the ground."

"That's what we said," Frank chimed in.

Jed gave him a dirty look and explained to Emmett why he hadn't burned down the town.

"So you didn't think anything of killing the sheriff and the mayor, but you wouldn't burn down the town because somebody might send a posse after you?"

"Kill a man and there will always be somebody who'll say he deserved it," Jed explained. "Burn down a whole town and people take it personal."

Emmett sat back and said, "Okay, maybe you're right. So what are we doin' now?"

"We're trackin' these wagons," Jed said. "It's possible that Lancaster and the ex-sheriff are with 'em."

"And if they're not?"

"Then we'll go back and burn down the town," Jed said. "Somebody's gotta pay."

Emmett thought a moment, then said, "Well, it ain't likely that a bunch of women and children would be travelin' alone, so I guess it's a safe assumption."

"It's the only one we got right now," Jed said.

"Okay," Emmett said, "so we keep goin' in the mornin'. Where's Johnny?"

"He should have been here by now," Jed said. "Boys, go and find your brother."

"Sure, Jed," Frank said. He and Peter got up and left the Red Garter Saloon.

"Still bossin' the boys around, I see," Emmett said.

"Somebody's got to," Jed said. "They can't make their own decisions."

"They can," Emmett said, "but they'd have to pay the consequences."

"Somebody's got to look out for them, Emmett," Jed said.

"Jed," Emmett said, "you looked out for us all our lives. Sooner or later a man's got to go out on his own."

"That's just what Sammy did," Jed said, "and he

Robert J. Randisi

paid the consequences, and now we have to deal with consequences because he was our brother."

"I get it, Jed," Emmett said. "I know you raised us all; I know Sammy was the baby—"

"I'd do the same for any of you," Jed said.

"You need a fresh beer." Emmett went to the bar and came back with a cold beer. He put it in front of Jed, who ignored it.

"I know the name Lancaster," Jed said. "Where do I know it from?"

"A while back he hired out his gun to anyone who could pay," Emmett said.

"Was he good?"

"Real good."

"Didn't he turn into a drunk?"

"He shot a kid by accident," Emmett said. "Disappeared after that. I heard he became a drunk."

"If he ain't a drunk," Jed said, "can we handle him?"

"I can," Emmett said. "The boys can't. You, I'm not sure about."

"Can we all handle him?" Jed asked. "And the sheriff, or do we need help?"

"We don't need help, Jed," Emmett said. "It's five against two. We can handle it. You thinkin' about the cousins?"

"I was, yeah."

"They're all idiots."

Their father had two sisters, one of whom had five

kids, another who had three, all but one boys. If they needed help they had seven cousins to call on, but Emmett was right, they were pretty much all idiots.

"Okay," Jed said. "Just us, then."

Emmett took a drink and Jed finally picked his up and took a sip.

"I wonder what kind of trouble Johnny's got himself into," Emmett said.

Chapter Thirty-six

Lancaster drove the wagon into Little Omaha and stopped in front of the livery. Jerry Ames came out and inspected it. It was little more than a buckboard that had been modified to carry the children from Philadelphia to California.

"Nice patch job on that wheel," Ames said, "but it wouldn't'a held much longer."

"I didn't think so, either."

"Well, I'll take it inside. Shouldn't take me too long to make the exchange."

"I appreciate that," Lancaster said. "I'd like to get back to camp with it tonight."

"Where are you camped?"

"Just outside of town?"

"Which direction?"

Instead of answering Lancaster said, "Guess I'll go and get a drink while you fix it."

"I can meet you over there—"

"No need," Lancaster said. "I'll be back here in a couple of hours. That should give me time to leave before dark."

"Still kinda closemouthed, ain'tcha?" Ames asked.

"Just a little habit I got into years ago," Lancaster said.

"Yeah," Ames said, "those old habits are hard ones to break, ain't they?"

"See you in two hours?"

"I'll have 'er ready."

In Fremont, Frank and Pete Quitman finally located their younger brother Johnny.

"He's in jail," they told Jed and Emmett, back at the Red Garter Saloon.

"What?" Emmett asked.

"Sit down," Jed hissed at them. "And keep your voices down."

Frank and Pete joined Jed and Emmett at their table. They both eyed their brother's beer thirstily.

"What happened?" Jed asked.

"There was a fracas at one of the other saloons," Frank said. "Sounds like Johnny started drinkin', and got into an argument with some cowboy."

"Over a gal," Pete ·tossed in.

173

"He pulled a gun on the cowboy but the barkeep bashed him over the head with a club, or something."

"A shilally, somebody called it," Pete added.

"A shillelagh," Emmett said.

"What's that?" Pete asked.

"A club."

Frank looked at Jed.

"Ain't that what I said?"

"Never mind," Jed said. "What happened next?"

"The sheriff came and hauled his ass off to jail."

"What about deputies?" Jed asked. "Does the sheriff have deputies?"

Pete looked at Frank, who said, "He had two with him when he came for Johnny."

Jed looked at Emmett.

"You've been in town longer than we have," he asked. "What's the law like?"

"I got here yesterday," Emmett said, "and I pretty much been in this saloon the whole time."

Jed looked around. The saloon was starting to fill up, but his eyes fell on the bartender.

"Frank, go bring the bartender over here."

"What for?"

"I want to ask him a question."

"What's he gonna tell—"

"Just do it!"

Frank jumped up, practically ran over to the bar and came back with the bartender in tow. He had the man by the arm, and released him when they reached the table.

"What the hell," the bartender said. "I got a business to run."

"We'll let you get back to it in a minute," Jed said. "Tell me about your sheriff."

"Whadaya wanna know?"

"How long's he been the law here? What kind of man is he? What are his deputies like."

The man narrowed his eyes at Jed.

"You gonna rob the bank?" he asked. "If I answer your questions you better tell me so I can get my money out tomorrow."

"No," Jed said, "we're not gonna rob the bank. I just want to know what kind of law you've got in town."

"Well, Sheriff Lawford has been the law here for a few years," the bartender said. "He mostly has to deal with drunks."

"And his deputies?"

"They come and go," the man said. "He's got two kids working for him now."

"How old's the sheriff?" Emmett asked.

" 'Bout forty."

"Was he a lawman before he came here?"

"I think so."

"So he's experienced," Jed said.

"I guess."

"Okay," Jed said, "you can go back to work."

As the barman walked away Emmett said, "An experienced lawman with two inexperienced deputies. I say we walk in there and get Johnny out."

"If we do that it'll have to be in the morning," Jed said. "I don't want to have to ride out of here in a hurry in the dark."

"We can probably get it done before dark," Frank said, looking out the window.

"I'll want to go and get a look at the sheriff's office before we do anything," Jed said.

"I'll go with you," Emmett said.

"Us, too."

"No," Jed said, "you boys stay here. We'll be back."

Jed and Emmett got up and Frank asked, "Well, can we have a beer?"

"One each," Jed said.

"And nurse 'em," Emmett said. "You know how you fellas get after two beers."

"Just look at your brother, Johnny."

Chapter Thirty-seven

Lancaster decided that he would kill time over a beer or two, but not at the saloon owned by Lloyd Ames. He rode down the main street until he came to another, smaller saloon, then tied his horse off in front and went inside. He guessed that the larger saloon got most of the business in the small town because this one was almost empty—which suited him just fine, at the moment.

"Beer," he told the bored-looking bartender.

"Right."

When the man brought the beer Lancaster said, "Not much business tonight."

"Or any night."

"Why's that?"

"The Ames place."

"I've been there," Lancaster said. "It's bigger, but"—he tasted the beer—"if anything, your beer is better—and colder."

"I know that," the barkeep said, "but don't say that out loud on the street. It might get back to them."

"And then what would happen?"

"I'd probably get burned out," he said. "I'm only in business because they let me be."

"I don't understand."

"What's to understand?" the man asked. "They own this town—or they will when it is a town. Before long they'll become the mayor, and the sheriff."

"Then why do you stay?"

"Where else would I go?" he asked. "I put every penny I had into this place when I thought I'd have the right to compete. I soon found out I made a mistake, but now I'm stuck."

Lancaster frowned. He knew something had not felt right about those two.

"My name's Lancaster."

"Bill Brooks," the bartender said, shaking hands. He was in his late thirties, and Lancaster assumed this was the first time he'd ever had his own business.

"I still don't understand, Bill," he said. "If they own this town why do all the people look so . . . happy."

"Because the Ames brothers want Little Omaha

178

to be a happy town," Brooks said. "The people here know what will happen if they're caught not smilin'."

"How would the Ames brother know?"

"There are more than just the two of them," Brooks said, "and nobody knows who works for them and who doesn't."

"And I suppose you don't?"

"0No," Brooks said, "I don't, and neither do the other men in here." Brooks waved his hand at the two or three souls sitting at tables. "These are the only men in town I can trust—and maybe a stranger." He leaned his elbows on the bar. "What brings you to Little Omaha?"

"I needed a new wagon wheel."

"And you're buying it from Jerry Ames?"

"That's right," Lancaster said. "He's putting it on for me right now."

Suddenly the other men in the saloon began to laugh.

"What's so funny?" Lancaster asked Brooks.

"Did you settle on a price with him beforehand?"

"Well, no . . . I didn't see that I had any other options."

"You didn't," Brooks said, "and that's what he's counting on."

"You're saying he's going to overcharge me?"

"Overcharge is a small word for it," Brooks said. "He's gonna charge you for the wheel—which won't be much—but then he'll hit you with a charge for his labor—and that's where he'll get you."

"I won't stand for it," Lancaster said.

"And what other choice will you have?" Brooks asked, "especially once the wheel is already on?"

Brooks was right. It wasn't as if Lancaster didn't have enough money with him, but it was the principle. How much could the man possibly charge?

"Better finish your beer," Brooks said. "It's on the house."

"You're not going to make much of a profit doing that."

"Mr. Lancaster," Brooks said, "I haven't made a profit since the day I opened."

Lancaster had a second beer—and insisted he pay for this one—and played a few hands of matchstick poker with the other three men in the place. They couldn't play for money because they didn't have any.

"We can't get jobs," one of them said, "because everyone knows we don't work for Ames."

"Why not leave?" Lancaster asked.

"The same thing happens everywhere," another said. "The powerful run things, and we either resist, or go along."

"This time we're resisting," the third said. "Full house."

Lancaster tossed in his cards and pushed back his chair.

"Time for me to go," he said. "Thanks for helping me kill time."

"Let's hope that's all that gets killed tonight," Bill Brooks said as Lancaster went out the door.

Chapter Thirty-eight

When Jed and Emmett Quitman entered the sheriff's office the lawman looked up at them from his desk, then cast a glance off to the side where two deputies were standing at a pot-bellied stove pouring coffee.

To the Quitman's way of thinking they were glad all the badges were in one room.

"You the sheriff?" Jed asked.

"That's right," the man said. "Sheriff Newcomb. What can I do for you?"

Newcomb was a big man in his fifties, with white hair and a white beard. Jed Quitman had good instincts about men, and this one would not be pushed easily.

"You got my brother in a cell," Jed said. "What do I have to do to get him out?"

"Your brother was about to kill a man earlier this evening, Mr. Quitman," Newcomb said. "I can't have that happening in my town."

"I understand that," Jed said. "Why don't you just give him to us and we'll see he leaves town."

"Well, there's the matter of a fine for discharging a firearm."

"He fired his gun?" Emmett asked.

"Only the quick thinkin' of the bartender over at the Tumbleweed kept him from shootin' a man," Newcomb said. "Your brother's got a bad attitude, Quitman."

"Sheriff," Jed said, "if you know who we are then you know we all got bad attitudes. This here's my brother Emmett, and I'm Jed Quitman. My other two brothers are in town, also. We want our brother Johnny out of your jail."

"I think you're gonna have to wait for the circuit judge to make his way to town, Quitman."

"And when will that be?"

"Shouldn't be long," Newcomb said. "A week, maybe two."

"We ain't got a week or two to wait around," Emmett said.

"Well, there's no need for all of you to wait," the

sheriff said. "Johnny's the only one in a cell. Why don't you fellas go on ahead and take care of whatever business you've got, and pick him up on your way back."

"We're not leavin' our brother in a cell that long, Sheriff," Jed said. "It just ain't gonna happen."

"Well, you don't have a choice."

"Oh yeah," Jed said, "we do."

He turned and walked to the door with Emmett in tow.

"I hope you ain't thinkin' about breakin' your brother out, Quitman," Sheriff Newcomb said. "That wouldn't be a good idea."

Jed stopped at the door.

"And what would you do about it, Sheriff?"

"I'd stop you."

Jed looked over at the two deputies, who were so scared their hands were shaking.

"With them?"

Newcomb didn't look over at the deputies. He knew what he'd see, and knew it would not fill him with confidence.

"With or without them."

"You'd stand against us alone?" Emmett asked.

"If I had to."

"Why?" Emmett was genuinely puzzled.

"It's my job."

"And they pay you enough to do that?"

"It ain't the money, Emmett," Jed said.

"What is it, then?"

"Pride," Jed said, and then asked the sheriff, "Ain't that right?"

"That's right," Newcomb said.

"See?" Jed said.

"Pride ain't much to die over," Emmett said.

"What else is there?" Sheriff Newcomb asked.

"There's livin', Sheriff," Jed Quitman said. "You think about it and you'll be doin' it a lot longer."

Jed and Emmett went back to the saloon, got themselves fresh beers and sat down with their brothers, who had half-filled mugs in front of them.

"Those your first?" Jed asked.

"Yup," Frank said.

"You told us to nurse 'em," Pete reminded him.

"What happened?" Frank asked.

"We run into a stubborn sheriff," Emmett said.

"You kill 'im, Em?" Frank asked.

"Did you hear any shots?" Emmett asked.

"Well, no—"

"Then I didn't kill him, did I?"

"Where's Johnny?" Pete asked.

"Still in a cell," Jed said.

"We gonna leave 'im there?" Frank asked.

"Just for tonight."

"You're gonna leave him in a cell overnight?" Pete asked.

"He deserves it for bein' stupid," Emmett said.

"We'll get 'im out in the mornin'," Jed said.

"Is that sheriff gonna let him out?" Pete asked.

"Likely not," Emmett said.

"Then what are we gonna do?" Pete asked.

"We'll get him out," Jed said. "One way or another, we'll get him out."

Chapter Thirty-nine

Lancaster walked his horse to the livery stable, thinking about what Bill Brooks had said. The man's words could have just been sour grapes, because his business was not as successful as Lloyd Ames' was. Likely the charge for the wheel would be fair, and Lancaster would pay it and be on his way.

But he couldn't shake the bad feeling he had about the two Ames brothers. He was just going to have to wait and see. . . .

When he reached the livery he tied off his horse, but before he had a chance to go in Jerry Ames came walking out, wiping his hands on a rag.

"My wagon ready?" Lancaster asked.

"Good as new," Ames said.

"That's great," Lancaster said. Then he took a deep breath and asked the magic question. "What do I owe you?"

"Well now," Ames said, frowning, "let's see . . . the wheel wasn't much, but I gotta charge you for my time and labor . . . two hundred dollars should do it."

"Two hundred?"

Ames smiled.

"Yeah, that should be about right."

"That's robbery."

Now Ames faked a frown.

"Now, now, there's no need for that," Ames said. "I gave you a lot of my time, Mr. Lancaster, to get you back on the trail . . . and you not bein' very friendly or forthcoming—"

"What's that got to do with the price of a goddamned wheel?" Lancaster demanded. "I didn't come here to make friends, Ames!"

"Well, like I said, we're a friendly little town," the other man said. "I'm afraid you'll have to pay the price for not bein' very friendly."

"I want my wagon, Ames."

The other man folded his arms across his chest and said, "You can have it as soon as you pay for it, Lancaster, and not before."

Lancaster's muscles tensed. There was a time in his life when he solved all his disputes with a gun. It took all his willpower not to draw it, now.

Ames must have sensed this, however, because he lifted one hand and suddenly Lancaster heard the sounds of the hammers being cocked on at least two weapons.

"It wouldn't be a good idea for you to try to take your wagon back by force," Ames pointed out. "After all, I did do the work, and you do owe me the money."

"I'm not paying you two hundred dollars for a new wheel," Lancaster said, "no matter how many guns you have pointed at me."

Suddenly, Ames became dead serious.

"There are only two, at the moment," he said, "but either one will kill you."

The man came closer to him, and didn't bother to disarm him.

"Which pocket do you keep your money in?"

Lancaster didn't answer.

Ames studied him for a moment, then stuck his hand in Lancaster's shirt pocket and came out with his money.

"I suddenly remember, from when you were in the saloon," he said, counting. "A hundred dollars even. Not bad. Now you only owe me a hundred. Don't come back without it."

Lancaster stared at him, every fiber of him wanting to draw his gun and fire—but at that moment it was not worth his own life to kill Jerry Ames.

"I'll be back."

He walked out, mounted up and rode out of town. . . .

"We need that wagon," Ben Lockwood said.

"That's why we're going back to get it," Lancaster said.

"Good." Ben took his gun out and checked it to make sure it was loaded.

"We can make do with four," Trudy said. "The smaller children can ride in the same wagon."

"No," Lancaster said.

"It's our worst one," she reasoned. "We'll move faster without it."

"While that much is true," Lancaster said, "I can't let this man take advantage of us this way—and I can't just leave that hundred dollars behind."

Trudy grabbed Ben's arm.

"Talk to him," she said. "A wagon—that wagon—is not worth one of you getting killed over."

"Sorry, Trudy," Ben said, "but I agree with Lancaster on this one."

"Saddle up," Lancaster said to Ben.

"Right."

"What about the law?" she said. "You could go to the sheriff?"

"There's no law in this town, Trudy," he said. "These two men control it."

"The entire town?"

"Well, it's not that big, and it isn't even really a

190

town, yet," he said, "but yes, the whole thing."

"If you and Ben get killed over this we'll be all alone," she reminded him.

He took hold of her shoulders and said, "We're not going to get killed. We're just going to get our wagon, and our money."

Suddenly, he felt someone tug at his arm and looked down. Aaron was there, looking up at him with saucer eyes.

"Don't leave us alone, Lancaster," he said, "please."

He crouched down and took the boy by the shoulders.

"Aaron," he said, "some men have done something to us that's very bad, and we can't just walk away from it. Do you understand?"

Aaron blinked and said, "No."

"Well, you will," Lancaster said, "someday. For now, just know that Ben and I will be right back."

"Are you going to steal something?" Aaron asked. "Stealing is wrong."

"You understand about right and wrong, Aaron?"

"Yes."

"Well, these men stole from us, and all we're going to do is take back what's ours. All you have to do is watch out for everyone until we get back."

Aaron rubbed his nose vigorously, thought for a moment, then cocked his head and said, "Well, okay."

Chapter Forty

Lancaster and Ben Lockwood rode to within easy walking distance of Little Omaha.

"This is not going to be easy," Lancaster said. "We've got to come away from there with a wagon, as quietly as possible."

"Not to mention our money."

"That'll be easier than the wagon."

"Do you have a plan?"

"I will," Lancaster promised, "by the time we reach town. Come on. . . ."

They crept within sight of the town, and the livery, and stopped.

"They've got to know that we're going to come for the wagon," Lancaster said. "Or, at least, that I will. You might be our element of surprise."

"So you figure they got somebody watching the livery?"

"They've got to."

"How many men do these brothers have?"

"I don't know," Lancaster said. "I know at least two had me covered, but there are more."

"Okay," Ben said, "you said you'd have a plan by the time we got here. What is it?"

Lancaster looked at Ben and thought, Yeah, what is it?

In Fremont, Nebraska, Jed and Emmett Quitman were standing across the street from the jail. Their brothers, Frank and Pete, had been sent to their room in the hotel. For all they knew, Jed and Emmett were also in their rooms.

"Still think we coulda used Frank and Pete on this," Emmett whispered.

"We can handle this," Jed said. "We don't need those two messing things up. This has to be done right."

"What has to be done right?" Emmett asked. "You still haven't told me what the plan is."

"The plan," Jed said, "is not for us to get Johnny out of jail, but for us to spend the night in jail."

Emmett stared at his brother and said, "Yeah, that sounds like a good plan, all right."

"Shut up," Jed said, "and I'll explain it to you."

*   *   *

After Lancaster explained his plan to Ben—explaining it to himself, at the same time—the other man said, "Well, I guess that could work. It's better than goin' in with guns blazin'."

"Anything's better than that."

"What about these other men?" Ben asked. "You think they'll help us?"

"If they're bored enough and ready to move on, they will," Lancaster said, "but let's go and ask them."

Lancaster led Ben through the darkened streets of Little Omaha to the small, second saloon in town which did not even have a name over the front door. Luckily, they hadn't gotten far enough in their development to light them.

"I sure wish we had some idea how many men these Ames brothers have."

"Maybe none," Lancaster said. "Maybe he bluffed me in the stable."

"You heard the hammers cock," Ben said. "You didn't get bluffed, Lancaster."

"Let's go around to the back," Lancaster said, and darted down an alley.

They found the back door, entered quietly and found themselves in a hallway. At the end of the hall was a doorway, and that doorway led to the saloon. From his vantage point Lancaster could see that the same three men were seated at tables, and the same man—Bill Brooks—stood behind the bar.

"It's clear," he said, and stepped through the door.

Jed and Emmett waited in a doorway across from the jail for the sheriff to leave.

"What if he doesn't leave?" Emmett asked.

"If he's as smart as I think he is, he won't," Jed said. "Instead, he'll send his deputies home for the night. If he does that, it still works to our benefit."

"So we walk in and kill him?"

"No," Jed said, "we walk in and make ourselves comfortable. Maybe even have some coffee."

"And then what? We spend the night drinkin' coffee with the sheriff?"

"There are worse ways to spend the night."

"And then come mornin'?"

"In the mornin' we get Johnny out of his cell and get the hell out of town."

"And the sheriff?"

"When the sun comes up," Jed said, "that's when we kill him."

Chapter Forty-one

"What are you doing here?" Brooks asked Lancaster.

"This is my partner, Ben Lockwood," he answered. "We're looking for help."

"To do what?" Brooks asked.

"We're going to get our wagon and money back."

Brooks leaned his elbows on the bar. The other men perked up to listen.

"Your wagon and your money? You mean he overcharged you like I said he would?"

"Yes," Lancaster said, "and he got the drop on me and took my money."

"He had help," Ben offered, in Lancaster's defense.

"I'm sure he did," Brooks said. "Look, Lancaster, I'd like to help you, but—"

"Yeah, I know," Lancaster said, "you've got your business to think of. I wasn't going to ask you, Brooks."

"You weren't?"

Lancaster turned and looked at the other men.

"I'm asking them."

"Okay, now," Jed Quitman said.

Half an hour earlier the two young deputies had left the sheriff's office. Jed waited to see if either of them would return, and when they didn't he decided to move.

They crossed the street, which was lit but deserted. As they approached the door both brothers drew their guns.

"Remember," Jed said, "no shooting unless we have to."

He knew Emmett would show the restraint his two younger brothers couldn't. If a shot was fired it would be because it was necessary.

Inside the office Sheriff Newcomb sat at his desk, wondering if he was doing the right thing by keeping Johnny Quitman in his jail. If he'd released him earlier all the Quitman brothers would probably have left town by now. As it stood, the potential for trouble was great as long as they were still in Fremont.

If he'd had older, more experienced deputies he wouldn't have worried as much. But the two he had—Troy and Marcus—were green. He'd sent them home because they were more likely to get killed than be of any help if anything happened. He'd been training them for months, but they were no match for a group of men like the Quitmans.

And the same was probably true for him. Once, maybe, he might have been a match for one or two of them, but that was a long time ago.

He stood up and walked to the wall where his rifles and shotguns were in a rack. It was unlikely they'd try anything until morning, but he was suddenly struck by the urge to sleep with his shotgun.

He was about to remove it from the rack when the door opened. . . .

Jed and Emmett Quitman entered the office with guns drawn.

"I wouldn't, Sheriff," Jed said. "Take your hands off that shotgun, and back away nice and easy."

Newcomb released the shotgun and stepped back. His gunbelt was hanging on the back of his chair, canted so that the butt of his gun was facing him. It would only take one quick move. . . .

"Don't even think about it, old man," Emmett said. "I'll put you down before you clear leather."

Newcomb locked eyes with Emmett and knew that it was true. He had no chance.

"This didn't have to happen, Sheriff," Jed said. "It's not like Johnny killed anybody. If you weren't so stubborn we'd be gone, already."

"Old habits die hard," Newcomb said. "Now what?"

"Now we make some coffee, sit and wait for daylight."

"And then?"

"And then we'll be on our way," Jed said. "Emmett, make some coffee."

"Sure."

"But first tie one of the good sheriff's hands behind him, to his chair—and move his gunbelt."

Emmett holstered his gun and did as Jed said. He moved the lawman's gun off the chair and tossed it to the other side of the room, then sat the man in the chair and tied one hand behind him.

"Why one hand?" Newcomb asked.

"How will you drink coffee with both hands tied?" Jed asked.

"That's very civilized of you."

When Emmett finished he went to the pot-belly stove and put on a pot of coffee.

"My deputies will be back soon," Newcomb said.

"We saw them leave," Jed said, holstering his gun. He pulled a straightbacked wooden chair over, reversed it and straddled it, facing the sheriff. "My guess is you sent them home for the night and told them to come back in the morning. By the time they get here, we'll be gone."

"And me?"

"Well," Jed said, "by that time you'll have both hands tied behind your back."

Chapter Forty-two

Lancaster and Ben left the small saloon and made their way through the darkened streets to the larger one, owned by Lloyd Ames.

"Wait here," Lancaster said.

He moved carefully along the boardwalk until he could look in the front window. Once he spotted Lloyd behind the bar he turned and went back to Ben Lockwood.

"He's inside," Lancaster said. "Are you sure you want to do this?"

"If you've come up with a better idea between the other saloon and this one, let me know."

"No," Lancaster said, shaking his head.

"Then you go do your part and I'll do mine."

* * *

Lancaster's part was to walk into the livery stable and hope for the best. Of course, he had no intention of going in the front doors.

He took to the dark streets alone this time and made his way to the stable. He went around behind it looking for the back door. When he found it, it was unlocked. He was sure it had been left that way for him. Looking around first—in case anyone was already watching him—he finally opened the door and stepped inside.

He had to pause for a few moments to allow his eyes to adjust to the darkness but then he could see that their wagon was sitting right dead center, with the new wheel on it. He had to shake his head because he sure as hell was not looking at a two-hundred-dollar wagon.

Now the plan was to get it out of there, hook up a horse or two and take it back to camp. Of course, there was also the matter of the hundred dollars. And then, even if they got both, what was to keep the Ames brothers from sending some men out to camp to get them back? In fact, if either of the Ameses was already smart enough to have sent some men out there, then the whole plan was dead because by now they had about twenty-four hostages.

Once again—as he had done from time to time since leaving Council Bluffs—Lancaster wondered how he had gotten himself involved in this hair-brained scheme to bring instant families to miners in California.

He just had to hope that they were not as smart as they were greedy.

It was time to announce his arrival—unless he'd already been spotted. He made it official, though, by finding a storm lamp, taking a lucifer from his shirt pocket, and lighting the wick. The interior was immediately bathed in a soft yellow light, revealing what looked even less like a vehicle worth two hundred dollars.

He started toward the wagon, and stopped when a voice said, "That's far enough."

In Fremont, Emmett Quitman had made another pot of coffee and put a cup in front of the sheriff.

"If I drink one more cup you're gonna have to take me out back to relieve myself," Newcomb warned.

"You just say the word, Lawdog," Emmett replied. "I gotta take a piss myself."

"You can both hold it," Jed said. "We're not leaving this office until morning."

"There are some piss pots in the cell block," the sheriff said.

"That'll do," Jed said.

The sheriff shrugged and picked up the coffee mug.

"Where do you fellas plan to head when you leave here?" Newcomb asked.

"Now why would we tell you that?" Jed asked. "So you can follow us with a posse?"

"Posse?" Newcomb asked. "I just assumed you were going to kill me before you left."

"And why would you assume that?"

"Oh, I don't know," the sheriff said. "Maybe because you and your brothers have reputations as killers."

"You got any paper on us, Sheriff?"

"Not at the moment."

Jed spread his hands.

"We have no reason to kill you."

"I'll come after you with a posse," Newcomb said.

"For what?" Jed asked. "Makin' you drink coffee?"

"This is kidnapping."

"We didn't take you anywhere," Emmett said.

"You're holdin' me against my will," Newcomb said. "That's kidnapping."

"It ain't," Emmett said, then looked at Jed and asked, "it ain't, is it, Jed?"

"It don't matter," Jed said. He looked at the lawman. "You won't catch us."

"I'll try."

"But not for long," Jed said. "You'll get tired and stop. Now, if we killed you, there'd be a posse after us that wouldn't stop until they caught us. See the difference?"

Sheriff Newcomb paused. For the first time since they'd tied him up he thought that maybe—just maybe—there was a chance he was going to get out of this alive.

Chapter Forty-three

Lancaster stood still.

"That's a smart man," Jerry Ames said. "Toss your gun away."

"If I do that," Lancaster said, "I'll be in trouble."

"You're in trouble anyway," Ames said. "There are half a dozen guns pointed at you."

"I'll take my chances."

After a moment of silence Ames said, "Did you bring the other hundred?"

"No."

"So you came to steal from me?"

"I came to take back what's rightfully mine."

"You got it wrong, friend," Ames' disembodied voice said. "That wagon belongs to me until you pay me what you owe me."

"I want my money back," Lancaster said, "and my wagon—tonight."

"You're in no position to make demands."

"I think I am."

"And what makes you think that?"

"We've got your brother."

Another moment of silence. The voice sounded to Lancaster like it was coming from the hayloft. If there were other guns pointed at him he didn't know where they were. Nobody else was talking.

"You don't," Ames finally said.

"Yes, we do."

"Who's we?"

"You don't think I'd come here alone, do you?" Lancaster asked. "Why would I just walk in here alone, Ames?"

"Who's with you?" Jerry Ames asked. "How many?"

"That," Lancaster said, "would be telling."

"I could shoot you where you stand, you know."

"Your brother would die, next."

Ames took another moment to think. Lancaster hoped that Ben Lockwood was actually doing his part.

"What's it going to be, Ames?" Lancaster asked. "I'll trade the wagon and my money for your brother."

"Lloyd is at the saloon, tending bar," Jerry Ames said. "I left him there."

Robert J. Randisi

"And I left my friends there when I came here," Lancaster said. "They have him by now."

"They couldn't have just walked into a busy saloon and taken him out."

"Why not?" Lancaster asked. "Everybody's drinking and gambling and looking at the girls. Who's going to miss him?"

"He's the bartender," Ames said. "They'd miss the bartender."

"Anybody can serve drinks," Lancaster said, "and as long as the drinks flow, nobody's going to notice. Come on, Jerry. If you got six guns pointed at me like you say, send one of them over to the saloon to see if I'm telling the truth."

Nothing happened. Ames didn't speak, and Lancaster didn't hear anyone move. He suddenly got the idea that the Ames brothers may have been holding the people of Little Omaha beneath their thumbs by virtue of lies and misdirection.

Maybe nobody knew who worked for the Ames brothers because nobody did.

"You can't send anybody to check, can you, Ames?" Lancaster asked. "And there aren't six guns trained on me, are there?" No answer. "Is there even one gun?"

"I got a gun," Ames said, "and I'm aimin' it at you."

"And I've got a gun," Ben Lockwood said, from the darkness, "and I'm aimin' it at your brother."

208

Ben had come in the back door with Lloyd Ames, and neither Jerry nor Lancaster had heard them.

"Lloyd?" Jerry Ames asked.

"I'm here, Jer."

"He got a gun on you?"

"He does," Lloyd said. "He came into the saloon bold as you please and marched me out with a gun at my back."

"Alone?"

"He had a few friends come into the saloon first," Lloyd said. The men from Bill Brooks' place, Lancaster thought. They had decided to help, after all. "He didn't really need them though."

"That's because you boys don't have any men," Lancaster said. "It's just the two of you, isn't it?"

No answer.

"Ben, bring Lloyd into the light."

"Move!" Ben said, and Lloyd Ames came stumbling into the circle of light given off by the lamp.

"Toss your gun out, Jerry," Lancaster said, "and then come out with your hands where I can see them."

"I'll kill you first!" Jerry Ames hissed.

"And Ben will kill your brother, and then it'll come down to you and Ben, and since he's an ex-sheriff, my money is on him to kill you. Then he'll collect our money and take our wagon back, and none of the three of us will be any the wiser."

He gave Jerry time to think that over.

"Or like I said, you can toss your gun out here and then step out, yourself. And nobody dies."

"Come on out, Jer," Lloyd said. "It's all over."

Lancaster heard Jerry Ames swear under his breath, and then a pistol came flying from the hayloft. Luckily, it was not cocked when it landed, and did not go off. Jerry Ames followed, climbing down a wooden ladder and then turning to face Lancaster.

"Go stand by your brother, Lloyd," Lancaster said.

Lloyd walked over and stood slumped next to his brother.

"Ben, get our money from Jerry."

"Right."

Ben walked forward, keeping them both covered, and put his hand out to Jerry who, grudgingly, handed over the hundred dollars he'd taken from Lancaster.

"I'm curious, Jerry," Lancaster said, "about the other guns I heard cocked behind me last time I was here."

Jerry didn't answer right away, then decided he at least wanted credit for his cleverness.

"I had a wire in my hand that was connected to a couple of pistols. When I pulled on it, the hammers cocked."

"Very smart," Lancaster said. "You kept this whole town in line with those kinds of tricks?"

"After the first few," Jerry said, "they were too scared to do anything."

"Well," Lancaster said, "not anymore."

"Just take your wagon and go," Jerry said.

"You first."

"Huh?"

"You and your brother," Lancaster said. "Saddle two horses and go."

The two brothers exchanged a disbelieving glance.

"What?" Lloyd asked. "We got businesses—"

"You've got nothing," Lancaster said, "except what you can put on a horse."

"You're crazy," Jerry said.

"No, you're crazy, Jer," Lancaster said. "You can't treat people like this."

Jerry shifted his feet and narrowed his eyes. For a moment Lancaster thought the man was going to charge him.

"You can't do this," Jerry said.

"I'm doing it."

Jerry laughed without humor and said, "You're gonna have to kill us."

Lancaster cocked the hammer on his gun and said, "I can do that, Jer."

"Jerry," Lloyd said, putting his hand on his brother's arm to hold him back. "Don't."

"Lloyd, we can't—"

"I'm not dyin' for you, Jerry," Lloyd said. "Pick a horse and let's ride."

The coin was in the air on what Jerry was going to do, but finally he relented—but tried to save face.

"You won't get away with this," he said.

"Saddle up quick," Lancaster said, "before I change my mind."

The Ames brothers picked a horse each, complaining all the while that they had property back at the saloon, and in their rooms, but in the end Ben Lockwood walked them out to the street and watched them until they had ridden off into the darkness.

"Think they'll come back?" Ben asked, returning to the livery.

"Not without guns," Lancaster said, "and by the time they get any we'll be gone."

"Yeah, but if they come back after we're gone, what's to stop them from taking over, again?"

"We'll stop on our way out and talk to Bill Brooks and some of the others," Lancaster said. "Once we give away their secret I don't think they'll be able to sweep in here and take control, again."

"Okay," Ben said, "so where do we find some horses to hitch this baby up to?"

Chapter Forty-four

The next morning they hastily packed all the wagons and started off. The night before they had hitched the wagon to two horses they found behind the livery, and then Lancaster had sent Ben back to camp ahead of him, just in case the Ames brothers had found it. When he finally arrived he was relieved to find that nothing was amiss. He was also embarrassed when Aaron charged him and threw his arms around his waist, hugging him fiercely.

"We were very worried about you," Trudy said, then added for Ben Lockwood's benefit, "about both of you."

"Yes," Kate said, sliding her arm possessively through one of Ben's, "we were."

They bedded down, with Lancaster and Ben tak-

ing turns on watch for the night, and then were off
the next morning.

"We're on the old Overland Trail, you know," Ben
said, just before they left.

"Old?"

"Well, it hasn't been used as such for about
twenty years, thanks to the railroads."

"If we could get these women and children on a
train . . ." Lancaster said.

"They don't have enough money," Ben said. "Do
you know how much passage for all of them would
cost?"

"No, I don't."

"Well, I don't either," Ben said, "but it's got to
be a lot."

"Let's get moving," Lancaster said, "and keep
your eye out for trouble."

"From the Ames brothers?" Ben asked.

"From anybody," Lancaster said.

He had not been thinking of the Ames brothers
when he made the comment, but of the Quitman
brothers. Having to stop to replace the wheel and
deal with the Ames' greed and deceit had cost them
valuable time. If the Quitman brothers were on
their trail, then they were now that much closer.

But he didn't mention his thoughts to Ben Lockwood, or to Trudy or any of the other women.

He was, however, wondering what the Quitman brothers were doing at that very moment.

Chapter Forty-five

"It's gettin' light," Emmett said to Jed.

"Okay," Jed said. "Go get the boys, saddle the horses and come back here for me."

"What about him?" Emmett asked, indicating the sheriff, who had fallen asleep with his head on his desk and his hands tied behind him.

"Don't worry about him."

"How you gonna kill 'im?" Emmett asked. "A shot would wake the whole town."

"I'm not gonna kill him," Jed said.

"What?"

"Didn't you hear me tell him that?"

"Yeah, but I thought you was lyin'," Emmett said. "Jed, if we don't kill 'im he'll come after us with a posse."

"So what?" Jed asked. "What kind of posse? Two green deputies and some storekeepers? We'll outrun them easy."

"They'll follow us—"

Jed grabbed his brother's arm and dragged him to the door, away from the lawman who may or may not have really been asleep.

"Look," he said, lowering his voice. "We lead them away from the trail we're following, then we double back and pick it up again."

"We're gonna lose time."

"It don't matter," Jed said. "We'll catch up to them eventually. This lawman and his posse will give up long before then. If we kill him we'll end up with a federal posse after us, and they won't give up until they catch us. We could end up with somebody like Joe LeFors on our trail."

"I ain't afraid of Joe LeFors."

"I ain't, either," Jed said, "but we don't need him on our trail while we're trying to catch the men who killed Sam. Emmett, come on, you ain't as dumb as the boys are. I'm tryin' to do the smart thing, here."

"Okay, okay," Emmett said, nodding, "I can see that. But when we're done can we come back here and kill the sheriff?"

"When we're done," Jed said, putting his hand on his brother's shoulder, "you can kill all the lawmen you want."

*   *   *

After Emmett left, Jed walked over to the desk and looked down at the sleeping lawman. It would have been real easy to strangle him in his sleep. The man would never know what happened to him. But even a lawman deserves better than that, and this one had been around a long time, long enough to earn some respect.

"Come on," he said, poking the man in the back, "wake up."

The sheriff jerked his head up, eyes wide open, but he quickly oriented himself and sat back.

"Damn," he said, "makes you sore, sleeping that way."

"You been trussed up before?"

Newcomb laughed and said, "More times than I care to count."

"Sorry about that," Jed said.

"Where's your brother?"

"He's gone to fetch the others. We'll be heading out soon."

"You know I gotta come after you, don't you?" Newcomb asked. "It's my job—that is, if you don't kill me."

"I told you I ain't gonna kill ya," Jed said, "and you do what you gotta do, but with two green deputies and a bunch of storekeepers I don't think you're gonna keep a posse together for too long."

"You're probably right about that," Newcomb said, 'but I'll give it my best shot."

Jed went around behind Newcomb and untied him. The old lawman rubbed his wrists.

"Come on," Jed said, "we're gonna let Sam out of his cell and put you in it. I'm gonna have to tie you up and gag you, though, otherwise I know you'd cause a ruckus."

"Yeah, I would."

"Get the keys," Jed said. "The boys'll be here soon and I want you out of sight or they'll wanna kill you. . . ."

Jed was sitting in the sheriff's chair when Emmett arrived. Johnny was over by the stove, drinkin' coffee, sulking. He knew that Jed had left him in the cell all night and he didn't like it.

"Why didn't you let me out—" he started to ask Emmett, but Jed cut him off.

"Shut up, Johnny, and go wait outside."

"I wanna plug that sheriff."

"We ain't pluggin' the sheriff. Go outside with Frank and Pete, I said."

Johnny slammed down the tin cup he'd been drinking from, pushed past Emmett and went outside.

"Where's the lawman?"

"Tied up and gagged in a cell," Jed said. "The boys outside with the horses?"

"Yep."

"What'd you tell them?"

"Just that we're leavin'."

Jed stood up.

"We best get to it, then, before Johnny gets them all riled up about leavin' the sheriff alive."

"What about these guns?" Emmett said, indicating the gun rack on the wall.

"Leave 'em," Jed said. "Posse ain't gonna catch up, anyway. I know it, and the sheriff knows it, too."

Chapter Forty-six

Day Twenty-four

Lancaster was surprised by several things over the next two weeks. They traveled steadily and well, much more quickly than they had before. He couldn't believe that replacing that one wheel would increase their speed that much. It was more likely that they had become used to one another and were operating well together, which made the traveling much easier.

They ran into no further difficulty between Little Omaha and North Platte, which put them more than halfway through Nebraska. Lancaster and Ben had decided to bypass Fort Kearny. If the Quitmans were trailing them they'd probably figure them to stop in Kearny.

Now they were faced with what to do about North Platte—camp outside or drive in to restock.

As Lancaster reined in his team Aaron remained pressed against him. After the incidents in Little Omaha the boy had begun to stay very close to Lancaster—usually pressing right up against him. Lancaster did not have the heart to push him away, and it was rarely a problem while they were traveling, since the boy usually sat next to him. It only became a problem when Lancaster was the one who had to go for water or firewood. It was difficult to walk with the boy attached to his leg like a third appendage.

He'd tried discussing the matter with Trudy, but all he'd gotten from her was, "I've never seen Aaron become so attached to someone. He got along with Mr. Bristow, but not to this extent."

"Lucky me," Lancaster had said.

But as the days went by he and the boy talked a lot—with him doing most of the talking, pointing new things out, teaching him things he'd need to know if he was going to grow up and live in the west. He was impressed by what a good listener Aaron was. Not only did he listen, but he retained the knowledge, because from time to time he'd point and recite it back to Lancaster. And so the daily conversation became enjoyable for both of them, to Lancaster's surprise. . . .

Now he gently detached Aaron and said, "We have to step down, Aaron."

"Okay."

Lancaster climbed down and reached up for the boy. As soon as he set Aaron down on the ground the boy attached himself to his leg, again. Lancaster put his hand on the boy's shoulder.

Trudy stepped down from the wagon and came to join them. Moments later Ben was there, as well.

"North Platte is just ahead," Lancaster said. "We can camp here, or drive in."

"I say camp here," Ben said. "It's safer."

"I think we should drive in," Trudy said. "The children haven't been in a town in weeks. We need to buy them some new clothes, and we could bathe them . . . and don't we need supplies?"

"Yes, we do," Lancaster said. "Ben?"

"We can buy the clothes and supplies and bring them," the ex-lawman said. "And the kids can bathe in a stream."

"Well," Lancaster said, "we can give the other ladies a vote."

"Or," Trudy said, "we can just let Lancaster decide. After all he is a wagon master . . . sort of."

When Ben gave up his badge he had also given up being in a position of authority. He'd adhered to

Robert J. Randisi

that decision by agreeing that Lancaster would be in charge. Lancaster, however, had never truly exercised the point.

He did, however, suggest that they follow the Platte River on the north side so that when they reached this point they would not have to deal with the fact that the Platte split into the North and South Platte. Since they were already north of it they would simply continue to follow the North Platte.

But that would come after they left the town of North Platte.

"Taking five wagons down North Platte's main street might cause a stir," Lancaster said, finally. "We'd certainly be noticed, and remembered. I'm sorry, Trudy, but I think we should camp here. You can come with me into town and shop for the children."

"And me?" Ben asked.

"I think you should remain here and watch over things, Ben."

"Fine," he said. "Trudy can use my horse."

"No," Lancaster said, "we'd better take one of the wagons. We'll be coming back with supplies."

"Okay, which one?"

"The one with the new wheel that started life as a buckboard," Lancaster said.

"I'll change so I can ride," Trudy said, and left them.

"Trudy, can you take Aaron to Kate?"

"Of course."

"Hey, big guy," Lancaster said to the boy, "go with Trudy."

Aaron looked up at him and asked, "You'll be back, right?"

"I'll be back later tonight."

"Promise?"

"I promise, Aaron. Now go with Trudy."

"Okay."

Grudgingly, Aaron detached himself from Lancaster's leg and took Trudy's hand.

"Must be annoying havin' that kid attached to you day and night," Ben said.

"Not really," Lancaster said.

"You know the Quitmans might catch up to us here," Ben said.

"I would have expected them to catch up to us already, if they were coming."

"Yeah, well, don't take so long in town," Ben said. "I don't want to be alone here if they do show up. There's how many . . . four?"

"Five, I think," Lancaster said. "I know a little something about Jed Quitman. Didn't put him together with Sam at first. Don't know why, it's not really a common name."

"It's common, all right," Ben said, "but only because there's so damn many of them. Brothers, cousins. . . ."

225

"Jed's the only one I've heard of," Lancaster said. "He's made a bit of a rep for himself with a gun."

"Well, I've heard of Emmett, too," Ben said. "He's no slouch."

"And the others?"

"Probably like Sam was," Ben said. "Too damned big for their britches."

"If they come at us," Lancaster said, "we'll have to deal with Jed and Emmett first, then."

"Agreed," Ben said. "Might not be so bad if we had some more men, either. Anybody you know in this part of the country?"

"If you mean friends," Lancaster said, "I can count those on the fingers of one hand, and none of them are in Nebraska or Wyoming."

"What about Colorado?"

"I know somebody there," Lancaster admitted, "but why don't we wait and see if we get that far? We're only a little more than halfway through Nebraska."

"Our pace has picked up, though."

"Some," Lancaster said, "but we're not going to be outrunning anybody."

"If one of these boys was old enough we could send them back a few miles on a horse to sit and watch."

"Well, they're not," Lancaster said, "but the women are."

"You want to send a woman?"

226

"Kate's young and strong," Lancaster said. "I'd send her if I could trust her."

"What is it you don't trust her to do? You think she might run off on us?"

"Not alone."

"What do you mean?"

"Never mind—"

"No," Ben said, grabbing his arm. "I want to know."

Ben's grip was strong and insistent. Lancaster knew that he and Kate were growing closer, but he had no idea how close.

"All right," Lancaster said. "I wouldn't trust her not to throw in with the Quitmans if it would get her away from here."

"That ain't fair," Ben said. "Kate wouldn't do that."

"Okay," Lancaster said, "you've been spending more time with her lately than I have. You'll be here with them. If you want to put her on a horse and let her ride back a few miles, be my guest."

"I might just do that."

"Okay."

They stared at each other for a few moments, and then Ben said, "I'll get that wagon ready."

As Ben left he passed Trudy, who gave him an odd look. When she reached Lancaster he couldn't see that she had changed anything. She was still wearing the same dress she'd had on before.

"What's the matter with him?" she asked.

"He thinks I insulted Kate."

"What did you say?"

He told her.

"I think you might be right about her," Trudy said, "as much as I hate to admit it. But on the other hand, she does seem to be getting closer to Ben."

"Maybe she's hoping to convince him to leave with her," Lancaster said. "And maybe she was the one who had convinced those other two to leave, and not the other way around."

"So you're saying they might both be gone when we get back?" she asked. "I don't believe Ben would abandon Donna and Martha and the children."

"I hope you're right, Trudy," he said. "I sure hope you're right."

Chapter Forty-seven

Lancaster and Trudy drove down the main street of North Platte, kicking up dust behind them as they went—not that anyone noticed. The town was bustling with people walking the boardwalks, crossing the streets, taking their lives in their hands as there was plenty of traffic to avoid.

"What a busy place," Trudy said.

"They still would have noticed us if we'd driven all five wagons in," he pointed out. "We would have been the cause of a huge traffic jam."

They passed several saloons and hotels, every kind of store Lancaster could think of. He'd never been to North Platte, but for some reason he was surprised at its size and pulse.

Lancaster spotted the general store but there was

no way he could stop the wagon right in front of it. He had to drive farther down before he could find a place to stop.

"It's midday," he said. "It might not be as busy in an hour or two."

"Will we be here that long?" she asked.

"I assumed it would take you at least that long to shop," he said. "I mean, you will be shopping for you and the other ladies as well as the children, won't you?"

"We tried to take everything we thought we'd need," she said, "but yes, there are some things Martha, Donna and I need. But, for the most part, I'll be buying clothes for the children."

"Well, we can get out here and walk back to the store. By the time you have everything you need I might be able to pull up in front and load the wagon."

No one had paid them any mind as they drove down the street but as Lancaster lifted Trudy down to the street he was suddenly aware that people were looking at them—or at her. There were many men tossing admiring looks her way, and even some of the women stopped to point and stare. Trudy herself seemed totally unaware of it.

Lancaster thought her appearance might cause some trouble before they left town. Western men were, for the most part, respectful of women, but that sometimes changed when the woman was beautiful enough, and the men had had enough whiskey. In a town this busy there were bound to be a lot of men in the saloons, drinking.

Lancaster took Trudy's arm, guided her onto the boardwalk and they started walking back toward the store.

"What about you and Ben?" she asked.

"What about us?"

"Aren't there some things you need?" she asked, "I mean, we have all this money—"

"Ben and I have what we need," he said. "I'll be shopping for supplies, though. We need coffee and flour and we can buy some sweets for the kids. Aaron likes licorice."

"How do you know that?" she asked, studying him curiously.

"You've been riding behind us this whole time," he said. "You must have heard how much we've been talking."

"I have," she said, "I'm just surprised that you remember."

"He's been remembering a remarkable amount of what I've been telling him," he said. "I think it's only fair I do the same."

"You're a remarkable man," she said.

As they walked to the store she suddenly noticed that people were paying attention to them.

"Why are they looking at us?"

231

"They've probably never seen a woman as good looking as you are, before," he said.

"Oh, that's silly," she said. "Maybe they're looking at you. Maybe they recognize you."

"I'm flattered you think I have that much of a reputation," he said.

"So then you do have a reputation?" she asked. He knew she was frustrated by not having been able to get him to talk about himself more.

"I had one, yes," he said, "but that was a long time ago."

"A reputation as what?" she asked.

"Nothing I'm proud of now."

She shook her head and said, "You're the most infuriating man, sometimes. . . ."

"I thought you said I was remarkable."

"I did say *sometimes*. . . ."

When they reached the store they had to pause to let several women leave before they could enter. Once inside it was still pretty much shoulder-to-shoulder and even though they'd intended to split up it happened quite without their intention. She just waved at him and melted into a group of women.

He went the other way, to the end of the store where there were mostly men shopping.

"Is it always this busy?" he asked the man next to him.

"It's Monday," the man said. "Most folks around here stock up on Mondays."

Lancaster had lost track of the days and was surprised to find it was Monday.

"Thanks," he said, and the man nodded.

Lancaster spent the next twenty minutes with a clerk—once he was able to get one to pay attention to him—filling the list he'd made before they left camp.

"This is a good-sized order," the clerk said. "Do you have your wagon out front?"

"There was no room."

"Ah, yes," the clerk said, looking at Lancaster over his wire-framed glasses, "it's Monday. Tell you what, why don't you bring your wagon down the alley and to the back? You'll have to load it yourself, though."

"That's no problem."

"Okay, then," the man said. "Go and fetch your wagon."

Lancaster turned and fought his way through the crowd to the front door. From there he craned his neck, looking for Trudy in the other part of the store. There were plenty of women there, some of them blond, none of them as lovely as Trudy, but all of them in the way. He decided he'd go and get the wagon, bring it around back and then go looking for her again. She wasn't going to go anywhere in the next ten minutes or so.

He left the store and started down the street toward the wagon.

It took him longer than he thought to get the wagon down the alley and around to the back of the store. He couldn't back the wagon up, and he wasn't able to turn it from where he was, so he'd had to drive it on, almost to the end of town before he found a place wide enough for him to turn around and come back.

When he got to the alley it was blocked by another wagon, and the man from that wagon was going in and out of the store, loading the wagon. Lancaster finally decided to just help the man load, for which he got no thanks at all.

Finally, he was able to negotiate his way down the alley, and maneuver the wagon to the store's back door. After that was done he had to bang on the door for a good five minutes before the clerk appeared at it and opened it.

"Sorry," he said. "It's a madhouse in there. I've got your supplies stacked by the door, here. Load it at your own speed."

"I've got to come in and find a friend of mine," he said. "A woman I came in with."

"Well, come ahead, then. Just try and have the wagon loaded and gone in the next twenty minutes or so."

"Twenty minutes—" Lancaster started to say, but the clerk was gone, already.

It had taken him almost forty minutes to get to this point, and as he entered the store through the back door and made his way through the store room he hoped that Trudy was not worried about him, or hadn't gone looking for him in the street. If she didn't see him or the wagon she might panic.

Of course, she might still have been looking at clothes and never missed him at all.

Chapter Forty-eight

Lancaster couldn't find Trudy. He decided to go ahead and load the supplies in the wagon and move it, and then continue looking for her. Once he got the wagon back on the street he had to leave it several blocks from where they'd first left it. He didn't know whether she'd find it or not, so he set off in search of her.

He went back to the general store and entered. The crowd had subsided somewhat and he was able to work his way over to the section of the store that sold clothes for children and for women. He spoke to a female clerk in her fifties and described Trudy to her.

"Oh yes," she said, "a lovely young blond woman. I waited on her for quite some time. She chose some

very nice clothing for children, and even a couple of
dresses for adult women. She said they were gifts
for her friends. Such a nice girl. What happened to
her?"

"That's what I'm trying to find out. Did she have
a lot of packages when she left?"

"Why, no, she didn't take her packages at all. I
have them right back here."

The woman went behind her counter and came
up with several bundles of clothes, wrapped and tied
in brown paper.

"Are they all paid for?" he asked.

"Yes, they are."

"I'll take them, then, if that's all right with you,"
he said. "I'll put them in our wagon with the rest of
the supplies and then I'll keep looking for her."

"It's all right with me," she said. "Maybe she
went off with that other gentleman?"

He was in the act of turning to walk away and
stopped.

"What other gentleman?"

"There was a man in here with her—at least, I
thought they were together. They were arguing as
I went off to wrap these bundles for her. In fact, I
thought they were married, the way they were bick-
ering."

"Did you hear what they were arguing about,
Ma'am?"

"No, I couldn't make that out."

"Can you tell me what he looked like?"

"Oh, he was tall—a little taller than you—dark haired, rather handsome, and he had two friends waiting for him at the door."

"What did they look like?"

"Oh, young, tall, wearing trail clothes."

"Did they look like cowboys?"

"No," she said, "they did not. To tell you the truth they looked like easterners dressed up as western men. The clothes didn't suit them, if you get my meaning."

"I think I do. Thank you for your help, Ma'am."

"Don't mention it," she said. "I hope the children like the clothes."

"I'm sure they will."

Lancaster left the general store and picked a direction. If Trudy left with a man he had no idea who the man was, or where they went. But if the man had two other men with him, then chances were she didn't go with them willingly.

And the big question was, were these men Quitman brothers? And if they were, where were the rest?

He had no choice. Since, in his opinion, Trudy was a rare beauty, he decided somebody must have seen her in the company of three men, especially if they were pulling her along. He could run all over town asking people if they saw her, but he decided it would be easier if he had help, so he went in search of the sheriff's office.

He found the office with no problem since it was right on the main street, next to the post office. The second piece of luck Lancaster had was that the man was there, standing behind his desk. He was a tall, well built man with intelligent eyes. Lancaster hoped that looks would not be deceiving, in this case.

"Sheriff, my name is Lancaster," he said, approaching the desk. "I just got to town about an hour ago."

"I'm Sheriff Vaughan," the man said. "What can I do for you, Mr. Lancaster."

He explained about coming to town for supplies with Trudy, and that she seemed to have disappeared, or been abducted.

"Now, hold on," the man said, "no sense in going off half-cocked, thinking she's been abducted—unless there's some reason that might happen that you haven't told me yet?"

So Lancaster went on to tell the lawman what had happened in Council Bluffs, and how he and the ex-sheriff of that town had ended up traveling with a wagon load of women and children.

"And this lady, Miss—"

"Bennett."

"Miss Bennett, is in charge of that group?"

"Yes."

"So it's not likely she just . . . wandered off?"

"No," Lancaster said, "not likely. She's too responsible for that. It's more likely that, somehow, the Quitman brothers beat us here and grabbed her."

"How would they know who she was?"

"I don't know," Lancaster said, "maybe they saw us together."

"How would they know who you were?"

"I don't know," Lancaster said, again. He was becoming agitated. He didn't want the man to ask questions, he wanted him to organize a search.

"Mr. Lancaster," Sheriff Vaughan said, "I have to tell you that I recognize both your name, and the name Quitman. I don't want my town to become a stage for some kind of showdown."

"Neither do I," Lancaster said. "There's also a possibility that these men were not the Quitman brothers."

"I think I'd prefer that, but then who would they be?"

"I don't—" He caught himself before he used that phrase again. "Maybe they were just three men who were taken with her."

"Yes, you commented on how pretty she is."

"Beautiful, is the word."

240

"Well, pretty gals are pretty common," Vaughan said, "but beautiful ones are kind of rare."

"So could we get out there and start looking for her?" Lancaster asked, impatiently.

"I suggest you go find a table at one of our saloons and leave this to me and my deputies," Vaughan said. "I'll organize a proper search and let you know when we find her."

"I don't think I'll be able to just sit and wait," Lancaster said, "so if you don't mind, I'll just keep walking around town. I'll check in with you, later."

"Were you planning on staying in town? In a hotel, perhaps?" the sheriff asked.

"No," Lancaster said, "we were going to go right back tonight—we had hoped before dark. I guess that plan is shot to hell, now."

"This ex-lawman, Lockwood?" Vaughan said. "He's out there with those women and children, alone?"

"I know what you're getting at, Sheriff," Lancaster said, "but there's no way I can leave town without knowing what happened to Trudy Bennett."

"Well," Vaughan said, scratching his chin, "I guess I can understand that. All right, I might as well get started."

"Thank you," Lancaster said, and started for the door.

241

"Lancaster."

He stopped at the door and looked at the lawman.

"If you find them," the sheriff warned, "I'd like for your gun to remain in your holster."

"So would I, Sheriff," Lancaster said, sincerely, "so would I."

Chapter Forty-nine

Lancaster combed North Platte for the next hour, talking to strangers, some of whom were wary of him. He knew that the amount of danger Trudy was in depended on whether these men were the Quitman boys or, like the lady in the store had said, men who were dressed like cowboys, but who weren't what they seemed.

If they were the Quitmans they'd probably get word to the camp that they had Trudy and try to trade her for the man—or men—who killed their brother.

If they weren't the Quitmans they'd . . . what? Take her someplace where they could rape her? Away from town? A hotel room?

A livery stable.

It had been a couple of hours since Trudy went missing. If they were going to rape her they had probably done it already. He decided to check all the livery stables in town, just in case. If they were done with her maybe they'd left her there, and he could get her to a doctor.

"Excuse me," he said, to a passing man.

"Yeah?" The man gave him a suspicious look up and down.

"How many livery stables are there in town?"

"Two," the man replied. "One at the north end of town, and one at the south."

"Which one's the biggest?"

"North." The man pointed, just in case Lancaster was too stupid to know north from south.

"Thanks."

Great. If she wasn't at one he was going to have to hightail it all the way through town to the other. He wished now he'd been smart enough to tie his horse to the back of their wagon. . . .

He went to the small one first, south of town. If he was going to drag a woman to a stable he'd choose a small, less busy one, where he could use a hay bed at his leisure.

Jesus, was he really trying to think like a rapist.

He found the entire south end of town to be the quietest. Or maybe it was just busy on Tuesdays or Thursdays. Whatever the case, it wasn't busy now, and as soon as he approached the stable he could hear the voices—a woman, and more than one man.

". . . told you I didn't want to have anything to do with you, Liam," the woman said, "and I meant it!"

"For Chrissake, are we gonna do this or not?" a man asked. "We've been dicking around here for over an hour. I didn't come all this way not to do it, Liam."

"Shut up!" another man said. Lancaster assumed this was Liam. "Just let me think."

"What is there to think about, Liam?" the woman asked. "Just let me go."

The woman was undeniably Trudy Bennett, and Lancaster had heard enough.

He stepped into the livery and saw them, three men surrounding Trudy. They all wore trail clothes that had never been touched by a speck of dust. Likewise, their gun belt leather gleamed, and the handles of their guns were adorned with either pearl or silver. Two wore spotless white hats, and one black. They looked like they belonged on a stage, somewhere.

"Hold it!" he said, loudly.

All three men turned and their hands fumbled for their guns. Lancaster drew his swiftly and all three men stopped and gaped.

"No!" Trudy shouted. "Don't shoot."

Not only did she shout, but she leaped in front of one of the men, her arms held out.

"Don't shoot, Lancaster," she implored.

"What the hell is going on?" he demanded.

"I'll tell you," she said. "Just put your gun away."

He hesitated and studied the three men, looking for the first one he'd shoot, the one who posed the biggest threat, but he had to admit he did not see any threat there. All three men were still gaping at him.

"Lancaster," she said, "I promise you you're in no danger. Just put your gun away and I'll explain."

"I'd like these gents to drop their guns to the floor, first," Lancaster said. "Then I'll holster my own."

She turned and said, "Liam, drop your gun. Tell the others to drop them, too."

Liam hesitated, then awkwardly removed his gun from his holster and dropped it to the ground. The other two men followed.

"There," she said. "Now please, put your gun away."

He hesitated, then holstered his gun.

"Damn!" one of the men finally spoke. "That was fast!"

Chapter Fifty

"What's going on here, Trudy?" Lancaster asked, again.

"Lancaster," she said, "this is Liam McCallum." She put her hand on one of the men, the one with the black hat. It was the only thing that differentiated the three men, as far as Lancaster was concerned. They were in their thirties, out of their element, and apparently impressed with him, at the moment.

"I know Liam from back east," she said. "He's come to . . . try to convince me to go back."

"By snatching you from the store?"

"He didn't snatch me," she said, "not exactly. I—I couldn't find you, and then I saw Liam enter the store."

"Wait a minute," Lancaster said, "Who are these other men?"

Trudy turned to Liam for the answer.

"Traveling companions," Liam said. "This is James and Doug."

Last names didn't matter to Lancaster. He was more interested in what they were, rather than who.

"Easterners?" Lancaster asked.

"That's right," Trudy said.

Lancaster moved forward quickly and all three men took a few steps back while he picked up their guns.

"What are the three of you doing with these?" Lancaster said. "You obviously don't know how to handle them."

"They—they were part of the outfit," Liam said.

"Outfit?"

"We wanted to dress like western men," James said, "to blend in."

Lancaster shook his head and threw all three weapons up into the hayloft.

"Wearing guns when you don't know how to use them is a good way to get killed."

"I want to explain—"

"No," Lancaster said. "Now that I've found you we have to find the sheriff."

"The sheriff?" Liam asked.

"Yes, I went to him when I couldn't find Trudy. I've got to call him and his men off, now."

"We can all go," Liam said. "This is a misunderstanding—"

"No," Lancaster said. "Trudy, you said you weren't going back with Liam?"

"No," she said, "I told him that. Back east we were—"

Lancaster stopped her with a raised hand.

"I don't need to know all that now," he said. "We're going, and these men are going to return to wherever they came from."

"Philadelphia," Liam said. "We took the train—"

"I said I don't have time for this now!" Lancaster snapped. "Trudy, we're going."

He put his hand out to her and she took it. He tugged her toward the door with him.

"Trudy—"

"Go back, Liam," she said. "I'm not coming with you."

"Go back, boys," Lancaster said. "You don't belong here. And leave those guns where they were. You'll only get yourselves killed."

Lancaster pushed Trudy out ahead of him and followed right behind her.

Liam started forward but James and Doug each grabbed an arm.

"She doesn't want to have anything to do with you, Liam," James said.

"And I don't want to have anything to do with

249

him," Doug added. "Did you see how fast he drew that gun?"

"But—"

"No buts," James said. "We're going back to Philadelphia where we belong, Liam."

"That man is right," Doug said. "If we stay here we could get killed. This turned out to be some adventure."

"It was more than an adventure to me," Liam said. "She's the woman I love."

"Well," Doug said, "you better consign her to being the woman you loved." He slapped his friend on the back. "It's time to go home, Liam."

Lancaster and Trudy went directly to the sheriff's office and found him there.

"Is this the lady in question?" Sheriff Vaughan asked.

"I thought you were out looking for her," Lancaster said.

"My men are," Vaughan said. "I just came back. Miss, are you all right?"

"Yes," Trudy said, "I'm fine."

"And the men who took you?"

"No one took me," she said. "Not exactly."

She explained to the lawman—and Lancaster— that Liam and his friends had come west to fetch her back to Philadelphia. Liam was in love with her, but she was not in love with him. When she left he vowed to bring her back.

"Now that he's tried and failed," she said, "I think he'll go back. I think all three of them were afraid of Lancaster."

"Then I'll call my men off," Vaughan said. "I'm glad you're all right, Ma'am."

"I'm fine."

"What will you do now?"

"We're returning to our camp," Lancaster said.

"It'll be dark shortly," the sheriff said. "Be careful driving back."

"We will," Lancaster said. "Thanks for your help."

When they were back on the wagon, driving back to camp, Trudy said to Lancaster, "Your thanks didn't sound very heartfelt."

"I don't think that man ever left his office," Lancaster said. "And I doubt his deputies were out looking for you."

"What does it matter, Lancaster?" she asked. "You found me. You rescued me."

"Did you need rescuing?"

"In a way," she said. "I think you frightened Liam and his friends enough for them to decide that this was not just an adventure they were on. You might have killed them."

"I would have fired, if you hadn't jumped in the

251

way," he said. "You must have some feelings for the man."

"I might have, once," she said, "but not anymore. It was you I was concerned about."

"Me?"

"I knew they were no danger to you," she said. "I didn't want you to have to live with killing any of them."

He looked at her, but she was staring straight ahead. Her profile invited his eyes, but he turned them forward, as well. It was dark, and he had to keep his eyes on the trail.

Chapter Fifty-one

When they got back to camp Ben Lockwood helped
Lancaster unload the supplies. Aaron and some of
the other boys helped, as well. Lancaster watched
Aaron and realized that, of all the children, Aaron's
was the only name he recalled. He'd traveled with
them all this way, and didn't know their names.

"We were worried about you," Ben said. "What
took so long?"

"Trudy ran into an old friend."

"What?"

Lancaster explained what had happened while
they finished unloading.

"Do you think they'll come after her?"

"No," Lancaster said, "I think they'll go home."

"Well, come on, then," Ben said. "You're probably hungry."

"What have you and the others been doing?"

"I'll explain while you and Trudy eat."

Ben explained that he had, indeed, put Kate on a horse and sent her off with instructions.

"She was great," Ben said, his eyes shining. "She was scared, but she went, anyway."

He was sitting across the fire from Lancaster and Trudy.

"What did she find?"

"Nothing," he said. "I told her what to look for, how to determine if anyone was riding toward us, and she saw nothing and came back."

"I'm glad for both," Trudy said.

Aaron came over and sat next to Lancaster.

"How are you doing, buddy?"

"Fine."

"Hey, I brought something back for you and the other kids."

"What?" he asked, anxiously.

"Well," Lancaster said, "I'll give you yours first, and then you can have the others come and get theirs."

Trudy went and fetched the bag of licorice they had bought for the kids and Lancaster handed Aaron two sticks.

"Wow!" the boy said, his eyes lighting up the way

Ben's did when he talked about Kate. "I get two?"

"Because you're my buddy," Lancaster said. "Now have the others come and line up and I'll give them each one. And maybe learn their names at the same time."

"That was pretty impressive," Trudy said, later.

Everyone else was asleep and Lancaster was on first watch. He and Ben had agreed to split watches in case Trudy's friend came back, or the Quitmans caught up to them. Both men were starting to feel like condemned men, one step ahead of the noose. They agreed that sooner or later they'd have to deal with the brothers for killing Sam—but maybe not until they saw the ladies and the children safely to their destination.

Trudy came and sat next to him, poured herself a cup of coffee so she could drink with him.

"What was?"

"That business with the candy," she said. "When did you decide that you had to learn the names of all the children?"

"Earlier today I realized Aaron was the only one whose name I knew," he confessed. "I didn't feel that was right."

"You could grow to love them all, you know," she said. "That would be a bad thing. Believe me, I know."

"Why is that?"

"Because I love them all," she said, "and I'm going to have to give them up when we get where we're going."

"It'll be better for them."

"Oh, I know that," she said, "but it doesn't help much."

They drank coffee in silence for a while, Lancaster listening intently to the sounds of the night. He was alert for anything—a footfall, the sound of a horse, the rustle of denim—that would give away the fact that someone was out in the darkness, watching them.

"May I ask you something?" Trudy said.

"Of course."

She reached into the fold of her dress and came out with a sheet of paper. When she unfolded it he saw what it was.

"I found this in the sheriff's office back in Council Bluffs," she said. "I don't know why I took it."

"Maybe you were curious," he said, looking down at his own likeness on a wanted poster.

"Perhaps," she said. "I gave myself the benefit of the doubt and told myself I was keeping it so the sheriff wouldn't see it—but now he's here with us, isn't he?"

"Well, then, their new sheriff won't see it," he said. "It doesn't really matter. It's an old one, anyway. It's from my past, so it's well out of date."

"It says you were wanted for . . . murder."

"That's right," he said. "I was."

"I can't imagine you ever murdering anyone."

"Really?" he asked. "Even after that scene in the livery stable today?"

"That wouldn't have been murder," she said. "You thought you were protecting me."

"Well," he said, "as it turned out it would have been as good as murder, so I have you to thank that it wasn't." He held the poster out to her. "Do you want this back?"

"No," she said, then, "yes."

He handed it to her and she leaned forward to put it in the fire. They both watched as the flames caught, turned it black, and finally devoured it, sending tiny remnants of it into the air.

"Do you want me to explain that?" he asked.

"No," she said. "I'm satisfied that you never murdered anyone in cold blood."

"I have killed men, though, Trudy," he said. "You have to know that."

"Why must I know that?"

"Well . . . if we're going to be friends—go on being friends."

"I know you killed men to save the sheriff," she said. "What else could you have done?"

"There were times in my past," he said, "when the . . . right of it might not have been so clear."

"I don't care," she said. "That's the past and this

is now. I quite like the man you are now, Lancaster."

With that she stood up, brushed off her dress and said, "Good night."

Chapter Fifty-two

Day Sixty

Weeks later Lancaster was surprised to see a sign-post that said they were ten miles from Cheyenne.

"I didn't think we were making time that well," he said.

"What?" Trudy asked, from behind him.

He pointed.

"Ten miles?"

"Means we've covered almost five hundred miles," he said.

"In how long?"

Lancaster tried to remember what day they had departed from Council Bluffs.

"Couple of months, I guess."

"Amazing. We never traveled that fast until you joined us," she pointed out.

"I'm not taking credit for this," Lancaster said. "To tell you the truth I'm shocked the wagons held together this long." All they'd had was the one broken wheel on one wagon. "I'm equally shocked all the horses held up." Not even a stone bruise to a hoof.

There had only been two bumps in the road the first half of the trip—Little Omaha and North Platte—but since then, the trip had gone remarkably smooth.

It was too damn good to be true. Ben Lockwood has said as much the night before, in camp.

"Somethin's gonna go wrong. It's got to."

"Maybe," Lancaster said, "we'll be free and clear once we're out of Nebraska."

"You think so?" Ben asked.

"I said maybe," Lancaster reminded him, because he didn't actually believe that, himself. He sort of agreed with Ben. Things had gone too smoothly.

Now Aaron patted Lancaster on the arm and said, "I knew you'd do it."

He looked down at the boy and said, "All we've done is make it through Nebraska, buddy. We'll be in Wyoming, soon."

"Can we stop in Cheyenne?" Trudy asked.

"I don't think we have a choice," Lancaster said, and started the horses again.

About forty miles behind them the Quitman brothers had made it to Kimball.

"Jesus Christ!" Emmett complained, leaning back in his saddle. "This wasn't supposed to take this long."

Frank and Pete slumped in their saddles. Johnny was anxious and couldn't stay still on his horse.

Jed turned and looked at the four of them, shaking his head. Things had gone wrong from the moment they'd left Fremont. First, Jed had expected to shake off Sheriff Newcomb and his posse within the first day, but somehow the lawman had managed to keep his people together for the better part of a week. They had not been able to head back south in all that time, and that put them well behind their prey.

Once Newcomb's posse had finally fallen apart and they headed south, Frank had let his horse step in a chuckhole. They were down to three horses after they shot his, and Jed had made Frank ride double with Pete. It wasn't until they had reached a small ranch house that they were able to replace the horse they'd shot—and they'd had to shoot the rancher to get it.

Jed didn't mind killing the rancher. Nobody was going to hunt them down over a rancher. He actually didn't mind killing lawmen, either, but he was willing to put that pleasure off until they avenged Sam's death.

And then Pete had stupidly turned his ankle on a stone one night in camp and it had swelled up overnight so that he couldn't travel. Jed had made him soak the foot in a cold stream for most of the next day, until they could finally get his boot back on.

"Cheyenne," he said, aloud.

"What?" Emmett asked.

"We'll catch up to them in Cheyenne."

"How do ya know that, Jed?" Johnny asked.

"It's a big town," Jed said, "and they've been movin' at a good pace to have gotten through Nebraska this quickly."

"Quick?" Emmett asked. "Shit, we been on their trail forever—and there's still a chance the men we want won't be with them."

"They'll be there," Jed said.

"How do ya know that, Jed?" Johnny asked.

Jed looked at his younger brother. "Johnny, just take it as fact that I know everything, okay? Stop askin' me all the time how I know things."

"Okay," Johnny mumbled.

"They'll need to rest in Cheyenne," Jed said. "That's where we're gonna catch up to them."

"We gonna take 'em right in town, law or no law?" Emmett asked.

"What do you think?"

"I think that's the only way we gonna let folks know you can't kill a Quitman and get away with it."

"Then that's what we're gonna do," Jed said. "We gotta send out that message,"—he looked at each of his brothers in turn—"and it don't matter how much longer it takes."

"Well," Emmett said, "if you're right and they're in Cheyenne, then it shouldn't take much longer. We can make Cheyenne by nightfall."

"We slip in at night," Jed said, "and we'll be ready by morning."

"Finally," Emmett said, under his breath.

Chapter Fifty-three

Cheyenne was quite a bit larger than all the other towns they'd encountered since Council Bluffs. Driving five wagons down the main street attracted attention, but did not cause a stir—even with the children hanging out of the wagons, looking at the people and the buildings.

Lancaster craned his neck to look behind him and saw two of the kids with their heads sticking out of his wagon, a boy and a girl. A few weeks ago he wouldn't have known their names.

"Annabelle, Jack," Lancaster said, looking back, "pull your head back in."

Jack, a boy of about eight, obeyed instantly, but Annabelle—six or seven—did not.

"Annabelle doesn't listen," Aaron said.

Lancaster looked down at the boy sitting beside him—who had been sitting beside him for most of those five hundred miles. Since North Platte, Aaron had stopped actually hanging onto Lancaster, although he was never far from him. After he and Trudy actually returned from North Platte Aaron seemed confident that Lancaster wasn't going to disappear, and started allowing some light to sneak in between them.

"Maybe not," Lancaster said. "It's probably because she's a girl, though."

Aaron nodded sagely.

Lancaster led the wagons to a point past the center of town where there was enough room for all of them to stop. By the time he'd stepped down, lifted Aaron to the ground and assisted Trudy down from the back of the wagon a man with a sheriff's badge was approaching them.

"Howdy, folks," he called in a friendly manner.

"Sheriff," Lancaster said. "Hope we're not blocking up your street too badly."

"Shouldn't be a problem," the fortyish lawman said, "as long as you're not planning on leaving the wagons here for too long a period of time."

"We should be moving out in a day or two," Lancaster said. "Maybe you can help us find a more convenient spot?"

"I'm sure I can." The man stuck out his hand.

"Name's Sheriff Boggs. Folks around here call me Jimmy Lee."

"Well, Jimmy Lee," Lancaster said, "this is Miss Trudy Bennett. She and her companions have come all the way from Philadelphia with about twenty children."

Boggs stared at Trudy for a few moments before he seemed to realize he was doing so, then turned to see Donna and Martha and Kate approaching with the children surrounding them. Behind them came Ben Lockwood.

"No men folk?" he asked.

"That's Ben Lockwood," Lancaster said, "formerly the sheriff of Council Bluffs, Iowa, and my name is Lancaster. We joined up with these ladies in Council Bluffs when conditions developed that left them all alone."

"I see," Boggs said, although he didn't actually. "So there are no husbands? Or fathers?"

"Sheriff," Trudy said, "all of these children are orphans. We're taking them to California where we hope to find families for them."

"Good God," he said, "you folks have been on the trail for . . . months!"

"Took us two months to get across Nebraska," Lancaster said.

"Doesn't seem as if you're outfitted all that well," the sheriff said. "Guess you were movin' along at about the pace of a good trail drive."

"Well," Lancaster said, "they didn't have very much money to outfit with. Thought maybe we might be able to upgrade here, though."

"Came into some money, did ya?" the sheriff asked.

"Some," Lancaster said.

"Well," Boggs said, "lemme see what I can do about helpin' you get settled, and then I guess you can do whatever business you wanna do in town." He turned to look at Ben. "Lockwood, you said? Outta Council Bluffs? I think we mighta exchanged telegrams a time or two, Sheriff Lockwood."

"Not a sheriff anymore . . ." Ben said, as he and Sheriff Boggs moved off to discuss it.

"He seems helpful," Trudy said.

"A little too concerned about our money, I think," Lancaster said.

"You don't think he'd try to rob us?" Martha asked, shocked. "He's the law."

"Just a thought, Martha," Lancaster said.

"I wonder if there's a place we'd be able to bed the children down comfortably tonight?" Donna wondered aloud.

"We'll ask the helpful sheriff about that, too," Lancaster said.

When Ben returned he said the sheriff had directed him to a clearing just at the far end of town where

267

they could conveniently put their wagons for a night or two.

"He also said there were enough folks in town who would be willing to give beds to the children, and the women," Ben added. "Cheyenne seems real friendly, for a big town."

"Why for a big town?" Trudy asked.

"Small towns just seem friendlier because folks know each other," Ben said. "So far Cheyenne sounds like a big town with a small town attitude."

"We've only met the sheriff so far," Lancaster said. "I'll reserve my judgment. Why don't we get the wagons situated and then we can look into those beds for the kids."

Chapter Fifty-four

They found the clearing the sheriff had mentioned, with plenty of room for the wagons. It was also surrounded by trees, and offered cover from the summer sun.

"Let's get the animals taken care of, Ben," Lancaster said. "Then we can take the women and children into town."

"Right."

"We can walk into town easily from here," Trudy said. "No need to wait for you."

Lancaster turned to face Trudy.

"I would think the trouble we had in Little Omaha and North Platte would make you more cautious, Trudy."

"But we've had no trouble since then," she countered. "And surely those men you were afraid were chasing you have given up after all this time."

"I killed their brother, Trudy," Lancaster said. "I don't think they're about to give up on that."

"Perhaps not," she said, "but they don't know who we are, and why would they want to harm women and children they don't know?"

It was clear she was intent on walking into town right away, no matter what he had to say.

"All right, then," Lancaster said. "Suit yourself."

And so Trudy, Martha, Donna and Kate took the children into town, where they could feed them, shop for them and even—perhaps—find places for them to sleep.

Lancaster looked down at Aaron, who remained at his side.

"You can help with the horses," he said.

"All right."

"Miss Bennett doesn't listen very good, does she?" Lancaster asked him.

Aaron shrugged and said, "Prolly 'cause she's a girl."

After they'd picketed the horses Lancaster considered briefly whether they should have tried to put them up in a livery stable. The others—even Ben Lockwood—may have figured nobody was on their trail anymore, but Lancaster was always one to plan for the worst—and the worst was having the Quitmans still following them. Putting the horses in a livery would have made it that much harder to hitch them up in a hurry.

"I need a beer," Lockwood said.

Lancaster would have liked one, too. It had been a while since he'd *needed* a beer—or, more to the point, whiskey—but there were still times when he would have liked one. Of course, that was what had put him in this situation, riding into Council Bluffs looking for one beer.

"Okay," he said, "let's go get that beer."

Ben didn't move, though. He looked down at Aaron, still standing next to Lancaster.

"Aaron worked hard, too," Lancaster said. "Aaron, how'd you like a sarsaparilla?"

"Wow, really?"

"Let's go," Lancaster said, putting his hand on the boy's shoulder. "We men have worked hard, and we deserve a drink."

"We sure do!" Aaron agreed, enthusiastically.

When Lancaster entered the saloon with Ben Lockwood and young Aaron they drew a lot of stares. Folks weren't used to seeing a ten-year-old boy in a saloon.

They went to the bar and the bartender stared at Lancaster like he was crazy.

"Mister, you oughtn't ta have a boy in here," he said.

"Do you have sarsaparilla?"

"Well, yeah, but—"

"This boy's traveled a long way and done a man's work," Lancaster said. Then he raised his voice. "Anybody in here begrudge this boy a sarsaparilla?"

The saloon was more than half full, as it was getting on toward dusk, and the patrons either shook their heads or said "No," aloud. One man even shouted, "Come on, give the kid a drink, Luke."

Lancaster turned and looked at Luke, a tall drink of water in his thirties.

"What do you say?" he asked.

"I'll give the boy a drink," the man said, "but then you gotta take him outta here."

"Deal," Lancaster said, "and my friend and I will have a beer."

The bartender set the two beers on the bar and then the bottle of sarsaparilla, which Lancaster handed to the boy. He took a sip from the bottle and then smiled broadly.

"Drink it down, Aaron," Lancaster said, grabbing his beer. "We've got to go and find Miss Bennett and the rest, so we've only got time for one drink."

After their drinks Lancaster, Ben and Aaron started walking up the main street and eventually they encountered Trudy, Kate and a few kids, including Annabelle and Jack, from Lancaster's wagon.

"Mr. Lancaster!" Jack shouted, waving.

Aaron, being ten, looked at eight-year-old Jack as a little boy, so he drew himself up to his full height and walked proudly between Lancaster and Ben.

"Lancaster," Trudy said, as they met up in the center of the boardwalk, "we've managed to place many of the children in people's homes where they can get a good night's sleep."

Lancaster wasn't so sure this was a good thing, for the same reason he hadn't put the horses in a livery. If the Quitmans showed up it would take too long to round up all the children. It was too late to do anything about that now, though.

"What about the rest?" he asked.

"One of the ladies told us about a boarding house up the street that is big enough for the rest of us."

"Us, too?" Ben asked. "I could use a night in a real bed."

Kate touched his arm. "We could share a room."

"You most certainly will not," Trudy said. "You and I will share a room, Kate."

The younger woman made a face and dropped her hand from Ben's arm.

"We'll walk with you," Lancaster said. "Might as well get us all situated."

As they started walking Aaron said aloud, "I had a drink in the saloon."

"Did not," Jake said.

"Did, too!" Aaron said. "Didn't I, Lancaster?"

Trudy raised an eyebrow at Lancaster, waiting for an explanation.

Chapter Fifty-five

A woman named Mrs. Macy ran the boarding house and she was happy to have the children there.

"I haven't had children in this house for many years," the woman said. She had white hair tied back and work-roughened hands. She looked six-tyish, but was probably ten years younger than that.

She went upstairs with Trudy, Kate and the kids while Lancaster and Ben Lockwood waited down-stairs.

"What are you thinking?" Ben asked.

"What makes you think I'm thinking anything?"

"Because we've been traveling together two months and I know that look," Ben said. "You ain't happy."

"I have the feeling that this will be the place."

"What place?"

"The place the Quitmans catch up to us," Lancaster said.

"And I got the feeling they're a long way away from here," Ben said.

"I hope your feeling is the right one."

Mrs. Macy came down and said, "I have a room for you fellas downstairs. Follow me."

She led them down a hall to a room with a single bed.

"Hope you gents don't mind sharing a bed," she said.

"We'll get by," Lancaster said. "Why do you have all this room, Mrs. Macy?"

"Because there are lots of hotels and other boarding houses in Cheyenne," she said. "Sometimes I'm busy, and sometimes I'm not. This is one of the times I'm not. I'm gonna make some food for all of you, if you don't object."

"No objections at all, Ma'am," Lancaster said. "Thank you."

She started to leave the room, then turned back and said, "Either of you gents belong to either of them ladies upstairs?"

"No, Ma'am," Lancaster said. "We're just hired help."

She nodded and left the room.

"Why'd you tell her that?" Ben asked.

"Now she won't have to worry that one of us is going to try to sneak upstairs."

"What about one of the women sneakin' down here?"

"Oh, a lady wouldn't do that."

Kate might, he thought, but not while he and Ben were sharing a room.

"I guess you guessed about me and Kate," Ben said.

"What's to guess?"

"I'm in love with her."

"She's a little young."

"I'm only thirty-two," Ben said.

"She in love with you?"

"I think so."

"For your sake, I hope you're right," Lancaster said.

"You still don't trust her, do you?"

"No."

"What about Trudy?"

"I trust her."

"I mean you and her."

"There's nothing between me and Trudy," Lancaster said.

"Are you sure?" Ben asked. "That ain't the way it looks to me."

"You're seeing things, then."

"Fine."

"We better go back to the wagons and pick up our saddlebags," Lancaster said.

"Ain't much in mine," Ben said, "but I'll come along with you to watch your back."

"I thought you said you were sure the Quitmans weren't coming?" Lancaster asked.

"I still owe you for what you did in Council Bluffs," Ben said. "If you think they're comin', I'll cover your back."

Chapter Fifty-six

After dark five men rode into Cheyenne and looked for the nearest hotel. As they started to dismount in front of it Jed said, "Johnny, you take the horses to the livery."

Johnny, in the act of dismounting, arrested the mood and sat back on his horse.

"Frank and Pete, take a walk around town and see what you can find," Jed said.

"What are we lookin' for, Jed?"

"Wagons," Jed said. "They're traveling in wagons, with kids, so find me some wagons."

"What if there ain't no wagons?" Pete asked. "What if they ain't here?"

"Johnny?" Jed said.

"If Jed says they're here," Johnny recited, "then they're here, Pete."

Jed and Emmett handed their reins to Johnny.

"We're gonna check in at this hotel," Jed said, "and then walk across the street to that saloon. That's where we'll be. You three boys'll be sharin' a room."

Johnny rode off mumbling, trailing their horses, while Frank and Pete went off to walk the town, also mumbling either to themselves or each other.

"I hope you're right about this," Emmett said. "I'm about plumb wore out."

"I don't care," Jed said, as they mounted the boardwalk and entered the hotel. "They're not gonna get away with killing Sam. It's as simple as that."

Inside Jed registered them all under their real names. He always did that because Quitmans were not ashamed of who they were. Also, it helped that they weren't wanted in Wyoming—one of the few states where they hadn't killed someone.

Jed got his own room, as did Emmett, and then they got one room for Johnny, Frank and Pete to share.

"Here are your keys, sir," the clerk said.

Jed took them without thanks.

"Do you need help with your bags?"

"Don't have any," Jed said.

"Would you like to see your rooms—"

"We'll see them later," Jed said. He looked at Emmett. "Come on."

"Good," Emmett said. "I could use a drink!"

After the two men left the clerk turned the register to check the names. The Quitman brothers may not have been wanted in Wyoming, but they were known, and the clerk—Les Williams—recognized the names.

Les rarely left the front desk unmanned, but this was a special occasion. And he wouldn't be gone long—just long enough to tell Sheriff Boggs that the Quitman brothers were in town.

It was Frank who found the wagons in a clearing west of town. Five of them, with five teams of horses picketed between two trees, and what looked like two saddle mounts, as well. He checked inside the wagons, but it was dark and he couldn't see much. Just enough to know that there was nobody inside. Not enough light to steal anything, and he didn't have any matches. Empty handed, he turned and headed back into town. Jed would be happy that he'd been right, and Frank would get a drink.

And maybe this whole thing would be over by tomorrow.

* * *

By the time Frank got to the Campfire Saloon Johnny and Pete had already joined Jed and Emmett at a table. He stopped at the bar for a beer and then went over to make it five.

"Well?" Jed asked.

Frank took a few swallows of beer before he put the mug down and said, "Found 'em."

Jed sat forward. "What?"

"Five wagons, twelve horses, including two saddle mounts."

"Where?"

"West end of town."

"Anybody in the wagons?"

"No."

"You looked inside?"

"Yes."

"Did you steal anything, Frank?"

"No, I didn't."

"Because if you did, you'll tip them off that we're here," Jed said. "That would make me real mad, Frank."

"Jed," Frank said, "I swear, I didn't take nothin'."

"All right," Jed said. "Okay."

"So what do we do now?" Johnny asked. "Let's go get 'em."

"Go where, Johnny?" Jed asked. "Do you know where they are?"

"No, but we know where the wagons are."

"Yeah," Jed said, "that's right, we do. So all we got to do now is stick around town, and wait. They'll come out onto the street sooner or later."

"How we gonna know who they are?" Pete asked.

Jed didn't answer, so Emmett said, "They'll be the two men with the women and all the kids, ya idiot."

Chapter Fifty-seven

Mrs. Macy had prepared them a feast the night before, and the next morning Lancaster came into the dining room and found another one. The table was covered with platters of eggs, bacon, ham, flapjacks, biscuits, marmalade, milk for the kids and coffee for the adults. The children were already at the table—Aaron, Jake, Annabelle and three others he was glad he recognized as Fred, Teresa and Lisa. Trudy and Kate were helping Mrs. Macy bring all the food to the table, even though the older woman was insisting she could handle it.

"You're my guests," she was telling them when Lancaster entered the room.

"Nonsense," Trudy said, "we're happy to help."

Kate kept silent, and didn't look as happy to help as Trudy did.

"Well," Mrs. Macy said, "that's all of it." She looked up at Lancaster. "You're just in time. Where's the other fella?"

"Ben will be along in a minute," Lancaster said. He had not yet strapped on his gunbelt, and had it over his shoulder.

"Are you going to wear that to the table?" Mrs. Macy asked.

"I'll just put it on the back of my chair, for now."

She sniffed, turned and went back into the kitchen.

"Sit down," Trudy said. "You, too, Kate. You can start eating."

"Finally," the young girl said. She sat between Aaron and Annabelle. Lancaster sat on the other side of Aaron, with an empty chair on his right. He hung the gunbelt on the back of his chair, where he could get to it if he needed to.

"What's all this?" Ben asked, entering the room. "Looks like enough food to feed an army."

"It is," Lancaster said. "Have a seat and help."

Ben started to strap his gun on.

"Uh, Mrs. Macy would rather you didn't wear that at the table," Lancaster said. He pointed to his own gun, hanging off the back of his chair. Ben did the same and then sat down in an empty chair across from Kate, who didn't look at him.

Mrs. Macy brought in one last bowl, filled with oatmeal, and set it on the table.

"There, you can all eat now."

"What about you?" Lancaster asked.

"I don't eat with the guests," she said. "Please, enjoy your breakfast."

"What do you say to Mrs. Macy, kids?" Trudy asked, seating herself next to Lancaster.

"Thank you, Mrs. Macy," they chanted, together.

"You're very welcome, children. Now eat!"

In the middle of breakfast someone knocked at the front door. Mrs. Macy left the kitchen, walked through the dining room and living room to the front door. When she returned she did not look happy.

"Mr. Lancaster, Sheriff Boggs would like to talk to you."

He exchanged a glance with Trudy, then Ben, then got up and retrieved his gun from the back of his chair. Ben started to stand, as well.

"No, keep eating," Lancaster said. "I'll see what he wants."

He slung his belt over his shoulder again and went to the front door. Boggs was waiting on the porch outside. He turned when Lancaster came out to join him.

"Mr. Lancaster."

"Good morning, Sheriff," Lancaster said. "What can I do for you?"

"You can leave town . . . immediately."

"Can I ask why?"

"We had some more visitors arrive after dark last night," Boggs said. "Maybe you've heard of them? Jed Quitman and his brothers?"

"Oh yeah, I've heard of them."

"Well, it's my experience that when fellas like you and Quitman find yourselves in a town together somethin' bad always happens."

"Fellas like us?"

"With reputations," Boggs said. "For using your guns."

"Ah." Lancaster figured his past qualified him to be lumped in with the Jed Quitmans of the world.

"So if you could get out of town before he finds out you're here . . ." Boggs said.

"Why aren't you asking him to leave?"

"I have a feeling he'd be less . . . receptive to my . . . suggestion."

"So it's a suggestion?"

Boggs frowned. "It's more of a request."

"And to pass this request on to him you'd have to face him and his four brothers."

Boggs frowned again. This wasn't going as he had planned.

"I only have two deputies," he said, "and they're not that experienced. I had to send my other three to Denver. They won't be back for a week or so."

"What is it with law enforcement these days?" Lancaster asked. "Is good help hard to find, or something?"

"Actually, it is," Boggs said.

"Are your men young?"

"No," Boggs said, "just new to wearing a badge."

"Well, I think you might have more of a problem then you think, Sheriff."

"Whataya mean?"

Lancaster hesitated, then told Sheriff Boggs what had occurred in Council Bluffs.

Chapter Fifty-eight

"You killed their brother?"

"Yes."

"And you led them here?"

"Well," Lancaster said, "we weren't actually sure they were trailing us."

"Well, obviously they were, and now they're here. And I only have two deputies."

"And me, and Ben Lockwood. That's five against five."

"I'm not joining forces with you," Boggs said. "I want you all to leave."

"Well then, you'll have to tell them, won't you?"

"No," Boggs said, "once you leave, they will, too."

"Sheriff," Lancaster said, "we have four women

and twenty children to load into five wagons. It's not like we can do that immediately. It will take time."

"Leave the women and children," the lawman said. "You ride out, both of you."

"We can't just leave them—"

"They'll be safe here," Boggs said. "They can even live here if they want. But you and Sheriff Lockwood have to go."

"That won't work."

"Why not?"

"Once we leave the Quitmans will grab the women and children," Lancaster said. "They'll hold them to make us come back."

"What makes you think that?"

Lancaster walked to the edge of the porch and stared out at the street.

"It's what I would do. Can you arrest them?"

"They're not wanted in Wyoming."

"That would have been too easy." Probably not, though. The sheriff and his two least-experienced deputies would have had a hard time with that.

"Look," Boggs said, "I can't have gun play in my streets. Innocent people will die."

"I agree."

"Then you'll leave?"

"No."

"Then you have some other ideas?"

Lancaster turned and looked at the lawman.

"Not yet," he said, "but I'm working on it."

Chapter Fifty-nine

Jed had breakfast that morning with Emmett in the hotel dining room. The other three brothers were still asleep.

"Okay, so what do we do today?" Emmett asked. "I want to get this over with."

"We'll send Frank and Pete to watch over those wagons," Jed said. "Somebody'll show up sooner or later. Maybe they'll even try to leave today. Whenever they show up, we got 'em."

"So we just wait?" Emmett asked. "Why don't we go lookin' for them?"

"Where?" Jed asked.

"Well—"

"Do you know what they look like? Lancaster? Lockwood?"

"Uh, no—"

"We could start checking hotels and boarding houses all over town, or we can wait for them by their wagons. They'll show up today, or tomorrow. They won't stay much longer than that."

"What if this is where they were goin'?" Emmett asked.

"Well, if that's the case," Jed said, "the women and children will stay, but Lancaster and Lockwood will still leave. We'll get them. Today or tomorrow."

Emmett rubbed both hands over his face, then centered on his eyes, probing them with his thumbs.

"What are you going to do after this, Jed?" he asked, blinking rapidly. "You gonna stay with those idiot brothers of ours?"

"What would they do without me?" Jed asked.

"Probably go to jail, or get killed," Emmett said.

"Exactly."

Emmett was about to ask another question when a man entered the dining room. He was wearing a badge, and looking around.

"Law," Emmett said.

"Just sit still."

The lawman spotted them, and came walking over.

"One of you Jed Quitman?" he asked.

"That's me," Jed said, looking up at the man.

The sheriff looked at Emmett, who just stared back.

"That's Emmett," Jed said.

"And your other three brothers?"

"Still asleep," Jed said. "What can we do for you, Sheriff?"

"Just wanted to stop by and let you boys know that I knew you were in town," the man said. "My name's Sheriff Boggs, and I don't want any trouble here in Cheyenne."

"Now why would we cause trouble, Sheriff?" Jed asked. "We're peaceable."

"You boys ain't wanted in Wyoming," Boggs said. "I checked. It'd be nice if you kept it that way."

"Well," Jed said, "I guess it'd be smart to keep at least one place we ain't wanted . . . whataya think, Emmett?"

"Smart," Emmett said.

"You boys stayin' in town long?"

Jed looked up at the lawman and said, "Just long enough, Sheriff. Just long enough."

Boggs went outside, where both Lancaster and Ben Lockwood were waiting.

"The other three are in their room," he said, excitedly.

"Good," Lancaster said. "Ben, you and the sheriff go up and get the drop on them. I'll go in and talk to Jed and Emmett."

"Alone?" Ben asked.

"You want to do it?"

Ben shook his head.

"I told you," he said. "My nerve is gone."

Ben had told Lancaster that just a scant half hour ago, when Lancaster had called him out on the porch to meet the sheriff and hear the news. . . .

"Damn," Ben had said. "They're here."

"All five," Lancaster said. "It might be better if we just go and get it over with."

"You mean . . . face them?"

"That's what I mean."

"Just the two of us?"

"The sheriff doesn't want to take sides."

Ben licked his lips, then said, "Lancaster, can I talk to you alone for a minute."

"You mind, Sheriff?" Lancaster asked.

"Hell, no."

Ben took his arm and led him to the other side of the porch.

"I can't," he said.

"Can't what?"

"Face the Quitmans with you."

"Why not?"

"Do you know why I turned in my badge in Council Bluffs?"

"You were upset over what happened—"

"Scared," Ben said. "I was scared, Lancaster. I still am. Almost bein' hanged . . . I've lost my nerve."

293

"Ben," Lancaster said, "you did pretty well in Little Omaha with the Ames boys."

"That was the last of it," he said. "I just about shit my pants that day. Look." He showed Lancaster his hands, which were shaking. "I'd be no use to you. I'd freeze up and get you killed."

"Well," Lancaster said, "I can't face them myself."

"Lancaster, I'm real sorry, but I got a chance at a life with Kate and I don't want to get killed—and I don't want to get you killed."

Lancaster thought a moment, then said, "Maybe we can keep either one from happening."

"How?"

"Just go along with me on this, Ben," Lancaster said. "Maybe we can get the sheriff to help."

Lancaster turned, walked back to the sheriff and said, "I've got a plan. . . ."

The plan was for the sheriff to go and talk to the brothers, find out if they were all together or spread apart.

"With those three upstairs asleep," Lancaster said, "they should be easy pickings."

Boggs and Ben Lockwood exchanged a glance.

"Come on, Sheriff," Lancaster said. "You won't have to fire a shot, and it'll keep them off the street."

"What about the other two?" the lawman asked.

"They'll be up to me to handle."

"Two against one?"

"I've faced worse odds."

"If you'd just ride out—"

"I told you," Lancaster said, "I'm not going to spend the rest of my life looking over my shoulder for them, and they're not going to forget about their brother getting killed."

Boggs thought a moment.

"The longer you wait, the more chance there is the other three will wake up," Lancaster said.

"Okay," Boggs said, "okay, if it's okay with Sheriff Lockwood, it's okay with me."

"Ben?"

They locked eyes—Lancaster and Ben—and the ex-lawman put his hands behind his back so Sheriff Boggs couldn't see them shaking.

"Let's do it."

Chapter Sixty

Lancaster gave Ben Lockwood and Sheriff Boggs enough time to find out the room number of the three Quitman brothers and get upstairs. Then he entered the hotel and made his way across the lobby to the dining room. He loosened his gun in his holster, took a deep breath and entered the dining room.

The hotel was called the Showdown Hotel. He did not notice the coincidence.

Jed and Emmett were about to stand up—had slid their chairs back, in fact—when Lancaster approached their table and asked, "Where you running off to, boys?"

Both men stopped short and stared at him.

"The name's Lancaster. I hear you've been look-ing for me. Should we sit and talk?"

"Lancaster?" Emmett asked.

"Mind if I sit?"

After a moment Jed said, "No, have a seat."

The Quitmans sat back down. Lancaster pulled out a chair and seated himself.

"You boys haven't been trailing me all this way, have you?" Lancaster asked.

"You with them wagonloads of women and chil-dren?" Emmett asked.

"That's right."

"With the lawman, Lockwood?" Jed asked.

"Ex-lawman," Lancaster corrected him, "but yeah, him, too."

"Then we been followin' you since Council Bluffs."

"Really? Since when?" Lancaster was still trying to give Ben and Sheriff Boggs time to get the drop on the other three.

"We got into Council Bluffs about five days after you."

"And it took you five hundred miles to catch us?"

Jed's mouth twitched. "We had some problems."

"Yeah, we had a few, too, but for the most part it was a good trip," Lancaster said.

"You killed our brother, Sam," Emmett said.

"Yes, I did," Lancaster said. "I'm sorry about it,

but he didn't give me a choice. He was trying to hang the sheriff."

"Why'd you butt in?" Jed asked.

Lancaster looked at Jed.

"I told you, he was going to hang the sheriff for no reason," Lancaster said. "I tried to get them to stop, him and his partners, but they wouldn't."

"So you gunned him," Jed said.

"I did."

"Then you got to pay," Jed said.

"How?"

"You gotta die."

Lancaster made a face. "That's too high a price, Jed. Maybe we can come to some other arrangement."

Jed shook his head. "You gotta die, Lancaster. You and the sheriff."

"Ex-sheriff."

"You both gotta die."

"You keep saying that," Lancaster said. "How do you plan to do it?"

"In the street," Jed said. "You and Lockwood, me and my brothers,"

"All five of you?"

Jed didn't answer, just stared.

"That hardly sounds fair," Lancaster said. "Five against two."

"You killed our brother," Jed said. "We all get to take revenge."

"Well," Lancaster said, "that's not exactly true. You see, by now your other three brothers have already been taken into custody."

"What?"

"That's right," Lancaster said. "Sheriff Boggs and ex-sheriff Lockwood got the drop on the boys while they were asleep."

"You're lyin'," Emmett said.

Lancaster looked at Emmett. "Go and have a look in their room. We'll wait."

Emmett looked at Jed, who said, "Go ahead."

Jed Quitman and Lancaster sat in complete silence while Emmett went upstairs to check on his brothers. Neither man moved, although the tension weighed heavily on both their shoulders. Lancaster wondered if he should make a move now, while he was alone with the Quitman brother who had the biggest reputation. Jed wondered if he should go for his gun now, while Lancaster wasn't expecting—except that a man of Lancaster's experience would always be expecting it.

So, in the end, neither man did anything, and they were still sitting that way when Emmett returned.

"They're not in their room, Jed," he said, "and the desk clerk said the sheriff and another man led them out of here at gunpoint. He said they were takin' them to the jail."

"We ain't wanted in this state," Jed said, "and

the boys didn't do nothin'. The sheriff can't hold 'em."

"He can hold them long enough to cut down the odds," Lancaster said.

"You like two to one better than five to two?"

"Just a little," Lancaster commented,

"Then you got it," Jed said. "Where and when?"

"Well, there's too many people on the street. How about that clearing where the wagons are? I'm sure you know where that is."

"We know," Jed said. "When?"

"Oh, I don't know," Lancaster said. "How about now?"

Chapter Sixty-one

They left the hotel together and started walking up the street toward the west end of town, where the wagons were. The Quitmans walked on one side of the street, and Lancaster on the other, each on the alert in case the other should go for their guns early. Word had gotten around quickly, and people were clearing the streets, finding vantage points to watch from.

But the town line ended just before the clearing, so that there was an expanse of ground that had no buildings, no wagons, no nothing—including no audience.

"Wait," Jed said, before they reached the wagons.

All three men stopped walking.

"What's wrong?" Lancaster asked.

"How do we know you ain't got men in those wagons?" Jed asked.

"I give you my word," Lancaster said.

"The word of the man that killed our brother?" Emmett asked. "What good is that?"

"My word's as good as yours," Lancaster said. "Make your decision based on that."

They did. Both Quitmans went for their guns. It had been a long time since Lancaster had drawn on another man. Back in Council Bluffs he'd started with rifle in hand, and then his handgun, but it had not truly been a question of who drew first. There was no time to think then, it was three to one, and if Ben Lockwood had not taken a hand—or a boot— in the proceedings, Lancaster would have been dead.

Right here, this was what he used to get paid to do, before that little girl with blue eyes had run in front of him and caught his bullet. He used to hire out to kill men and most of the time he did it this way, face to face, fair and square. Only it was never the fastest man who won, for if that were the case Lancaster would have been dead ten times over. He'd been outdrawn at least that many times, but he was always the more accurate shot, and that was how he had survived all these years.

He'd also survived knowing which man to kill first when he was outnumbered.

He watched Jed Quitman and when the two

brothers made their move Jed was the one who Lancaster concentrated on. Jed outdrew him cleanly, but the man's first shot whizzed past Lancaster's ear because it was rushed. He drew, then, and fired with surprising calm. He didn't think he had it in him any more, but obviously he did. He fired and his bullet struck Jed in the chest. The man's mouth dropped open as if he'd been punched in the stomach, but Lancaster had no time to wait and see what happened next. He turned his gun toward Emmett Quitman and saw that it was he who was the fastest, this time. Emmett's gun was just clearing leather when Lancaster fired a second time. His bullet struck Emmett in the gut, doubling him over, causing blood to gush from his mouth onto the ground, and it was onto that puddle he fell face first.

Lancaster turned his attention back to Jed Quitman and saw that the man was on his back, but his feet were still moving, trying to find purchase so that he could get up. His gun was on the ground right next to him, so Lancaster hurried to the man's side and kicked it away. He looked down at him and saw that he was only seconds from death.

"Hey . . . hey . . ." Jed said.

"What?" Lancaster crouched over. "What is it, Jed?"

". . . k-killed three of us," Jed said, his lungs filling with blood. "D-don't kill other t-three. . . ."

303

He was pleading for the lives of his other three brothers.

"I won't kill them, Jed," Lancaster said, "if I don't have to."

". . . h-harmless . . . w-without . . . me," Jed said, and then he died.

Lancaster straightened, ejected the spent shells from his gun, replaced them and then holstered his weapon. He turned to see not only Sheriff Boggs and Ben Lookwood running toward him, but also Trudy Bennett, little Aaron and—behind them— about half the town.

When they reached him they stopped and looked down at the dead men. Trudy examined Lancaster for wounds, but Aaron simply ran right into him, grabbing him around the waist and hugging him. Lancaster picked up the boy and turned so that the child could not see the dead men.

"Is it over?" Trudy asked him.

"It's over," Lancaster said, and walked away with Aaron in his arms.

Chapter Sixty-two

Day Sixty-eight

The railroad platform was filled with people, many of them children. Donna and Martha were trying to herd them, keeping them away from the tracks and out of the way of other people. They were all wearing new clothes, including the women.

Lancaster was standing off to one side with Trudy on one side, and Aaron on the other, affixed to his leg.

"We're going to miss you," Trudy said.

"I'll miss you all, too," Lancaster said, "especially my buddy, here."

"You can still come with us, Lancaster," Aaron said, looking up at him.

"I can't, Aaron," Lancaster said. "There's really nothing for me to do in California."

"We could be your family."

Lancaster looked to Trudy for help. How do you tell a little boy you didn't want to be his family—and it wasn't that Lancaster didn't want to be Aaron's family, it was that he couldn't be anybody's family, not at this late stage in his life.

For a moment he thought he'd get no help from Trudy. He had the feeling that Ben Lockwood had been right, that there was something between him and Trudy, but Lancaster was not a whole man, yet. His life changed drastically over the past few years, and he still had not decided who or what he was. He'd at least thought that he wasn't a killer anymore, but the past couple of months belied that as a fact. Shooting down Jed and Emmett Quitman had come too easy to him. He still had to deal with the aftermath for himself.

Once the Quitmans were removed from the street Lancaster had gone to the sheriff's office with Boggs and Ben Lockwood.

"What do we do with them, now?" Ben asked.

"Can't let 'em go," Boggs said. "They'll come after you."

"With his last breath Jed asked me not to kill them," Lancaster had said.

"You'll have to, if they come after you," Boggs said. "They trailed you all this way for killing one brother, what do you think they'll do now that you killed three?"

"He said they were harmless without him."

"I doubt that."

"I do, too," Lancaster said. "I think without him they might even become more dangerous."

"So what do we do?"

"Take 'em in," Boggs said, "and collect the reward on all five."

"They're not wanted," Lancaster said.

"In Wyoming," the sheriff replied. "Take 'em across the border back in Nebraska, to Scottsbluff or Kimball and turn them in there. The five of them are worth a lot of money."

And they were . . . they were worth enough to buy Trudy and the other women and children train tickets to California on the Union Pacific, which had a stop in Cheyenne. That was the train they were waiting for right now, and Lancaster couldn't wait to get them all on it, so Aaron would stop looking at him that way.

"Trudy."

"I'll talk to him," she said. "Come with me, Aaron."

She took the boy's hand and the other little hand reluctantly let loose of Lancaster's leg. Trudy took him off so she could talk to him alone. Lancaster was then joined by Ben Lockwood.

"I can't tell you how sorry I am," Ben said.

"About what?"

"That you had to go through that alone, last week." It had taken Lancaster the better part of a week to take the Quitmans to Kimball, collect the reward, and return.

"Ben," Lancaster said, "you found out a lot of things about yourself these past couple of months. I can't fault you for any of them."

"Which one you talkin' about?" Ben asked. "Bein' a coward, or fallin' in love?"

"Like I said," Lancaster said, "I can't fault you for nothing. You're not a coward, you're a man who can't live that life, anymore. And as for fallin' in love"—Lancaster looked over at Kate, pretty as a picture, waiting patiently for the train to pull in, a young woman he still didn't trust. "I wish you the best of luck, Ben."

The two men shook hands and then the children began to shout because the train was pulling in. . . .

It took a while to get them all loaded and seated in the car. And the last ones to climb aboard were Trudy and Aaron.

"Thank you for everything," Trudy said. She hugged him, and kissed his cheek. He thought that the way she smelled that day would stay with him for a long time.

"Good luck, Trudy," he said. "I hope you find what you're looking for."

"I hope you do, too, Lancaster."

He crouched down level with Aaron.

"Good-bye, little man. You be good, you hear?"

Aaron kept his eyes down, but at the last minute lifted them, then threw his arms around Lancaster's neck and hugged him tightly.

There was much unspoken love in the boy's hug, and Lancaster was grateful it was unspoken.

" 'Bye, Lancaster."

Lancaster just hugged him back for a moment, unable to speak, then released him and watched as he and Trudy boarded the train.

MIRACLE
OF THE
JACAL
ROBERT J. RANDISI

Elfego Baca is a young lawman—but he already has a reputation. He is known to be good with a gun. Very good. And he is known to never back down, especially if he is fighting for something he believes in. This reputation has spread far and wide throughout his home territory of New Mexico. Sometimes it works in his favor, sometimes it works against him. But there will come a day when his reputation will not only be tested, but expanded—a day when young Elfego will have to prove just how good with a gun he really is . . . and how brave. It will be a day when he will have to do the impossible and live through it. For a long time afterward, people will still be talking about the miracle of the *jacal*.

___4923-6 $4.99 US/$5.99 CAN

Dorchester Publishing Co., Inc.
P.O. Box 6640
Wayne, PA 19087-8640

GUNS IN
THE DESERT
LAURAN PAINE

This volume collects two exciting Lauran Paine Westerns in one book! In *The Silent Outcast*, Caleb Doorn is scouting for the U.S. Army when a small wagon train passes on its way to California. The train's path will take its members through Blackfoot country and the wagon master has foolishly taken a Blackfoot girl hostage. . . . In the title tale, Johnny Wilton, the youngest member of the Wilton gang, is shot and killed while attempting to set fire to the town. The surviving members of the gang plan a simple revenge—attack the town and kill everyone in it!

Dorchester Publishing Co., Inc.
P.O. Box 6640 _____ 5262-8
Wayne, PA 19087-8640 $4.99 US/$6.99 CAN